D1136292

Lal and Lucy looked at Mac, then at me.

"OH YES. ME. Um. I am . . . Becca. Yes. I don't normally go round kicking trees and snogging strange boys, you know. . . ."

"Don't tell me that you snog trees and kick boys," said Lal, and Mac and Lucy laughed.

I gave Lal a filthy look.

"Sorry," said Lal with a big grin. "I interrupted. You were saying?"

"I was saying—or at least trying to say—that I am quite normal, really. Honestly, I am. Not mad at all."

"Shame," said Lal, "because I like mad girls. They make life interesting."

And then he held eye contact for a few moments and I felt my stomach do that leapy-lurch thing that it does when there is fanciability in the air. *Hmmm,* I thought. *Maybe I'm not quite through with boys just yet. . . .*

Also by Cathy Hopkins:

MATES, DATES, AND INFLATABLE BRAS

MATES, DATES, AND COSMIC KISSES

MATES, DATES, AND DESIGNER DIVAS

MATES, DATES, AND SLEEPOVER SECRETS

MATES, DATES, AND SOLE SURVIVORS

MATES, DATES, AND MAD MISTAKES

MATES, DATES, AND SEQUIN SMILES

MATES, DATES, AND TEMPTING TROUBLE

MATES, DATES, AND GREAT ESCAPES

MATES, DATES, AND CHOCOLATE CHEATS

MATES, DATES, AND DIAMOND DESTINY

MATES, DATES, AND SIZZLING SUMMERS

THE MATES, DATES GUIDE TO LIFE, LOVE,
AND LOOKING LUSCIOUS

WHITE LIES AND BAREFACED TRUTHS

THE PRINCESS OF POP

TEEN QUEENS AND HAS-BEENS

STARSTRUCK

DOUBLE DARE

MIDSUMMER MELTDOWN

LOVE LOTTERY

available from Simon Pulse
published by Simon & Schuster

Love Lottery

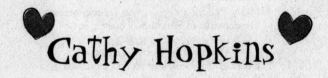

Cathy Hopkins

Simon Pulse
New York · London · Toronto · Sydney

If you purchased this book without a cover, you should be aware that this book is stolen property. It was reported as "unsold and destroyed" to the publisher, and neither the author nor the publisher has received any payment for this "stripped book."

This book is a work of fiction. Any references to historical events, real people, or real locales are used fictitiously. Other names, characters, places, and incidents are the product of the author's imagination, and any resemblance to actual events or locales or persons, living or dead, is entirely coincidental.

SIMON PULSE
An imprint of Simon & Schuster
Children's Publishing Division
1230 Avenue of the Americas, New York, NY 10020

Copyright © 2006 by Cathy Hopkins
Originally published in Great Britain in 2006
by Picadilly Press, Ltd.
Published by arrangement with Picadilly Press Ltd.
All rights reserved, including the right of reproduction in
whole or in part in any form.

SIMON PULSE and colophon are registered
trademarks of Simon & Schuster, Inc.

Designed by Debra Sfetsios
The text of this book was set in Garamond 3.

Manufactured in the United States of America
First Simon Pulse edition December 2006
2 4 6 8 10 9 7 5 3 1

Library of Congress Control Number 2006921276
ISBN-13: 978-1-4169-2721-1
ISBN-10: 0-4169-2721-2

*Big thanks to Brenda Gardner, Melissa Patey,
and all the fab team at Piccadilly. And thanks as always
to Steve Lovering for all his support and help,
especially in accompanying me to all the locations
in the books and taking photos of them.*

truth or dare

Love Lottery

All Hail My Fellow Nutters ♡ 1

"SCHOOL'S OUT FOR SUMMER!" I sang from the aisle at the front of the bus while waving my arms up in the air à la rock-concert style.

"Schooooool's out for summer!" echoed half the bus, including my mates Lia, Cat, Squidge, and Mac, who were sitting in a line on the back row. Even Mr. McKee, the bus driver, joined in with gusto. Usually he's Mr. Grumpypoo and would have asked me to sit down and shut up ages ago. He clearly welcomed the upcoming break as much as the rest of us. The non-singers were mainly old-age pensioners traveling back from shopping in Torpoint. Most of them smiled meekly and did that rolling-the-eyes thing to each other, meaning, *Ohhhhhhh, the youth of today! What are they like?! And don't you wish they'd shut up?*

Squidge and Mac had actually broken up a couple of weeks earlier than the rest of us as they were both in

Year Eleven and had been doing their GSCEs whereas Cat, Lia, and I have just finished Year Nine. We were all in today, though, because our headmistress, Mrs. Peterson, had insisted that everyone attended the last day to tidy up, return library books, and so on.

"Six whole weeks without lessons," Cat said, grinning as I made my way down the aisle to the back and swung in to sit next to her when the singing session had ended. "Without homework. Without having to get up in the morning. Yippity-doo-daa-yippity-ay. Life doesn't get much better than this."

"Six whole weeks to hang out at Whitsand Beach with you guys," I said, "checking out the tourist talent. We've got the Maker Festival at the end of July so loads of people will come for that, but before then it's going to be sun, sea, and shopping. I have to look my tip-top best for the festival so I'll have to find an outfit."

Musicians come from all over the country to play at the Maker Festival and this year I was going to be one of the featured artists. I couldn't wait. It was going to be the highlight of the summer for me, because although yes, I was glad to be on holiday, another part of me was dreading the coming weeks. I planned to spend as much time as possible outdoors, away from home and away from the uncomfortable atmosphere that there had been between my parents lately. Their constant bickering was doing my head in. I figured it shouldn't be difficult getting out a lot as most people down here do exactly that in the summer—boating, swimming, sunbathing, surfing, hiking, picnicking. The area where we live is called the Rame Peninsula; it's in Cornwall and from May to September it is flooded with tourists. It makes a refreshing change for us locals as, the rest of the year, the place is like a ghost town. Pretty and quaint, but quiet. Everyone knows everyone else's business and passes it round, as there's nothing else to do. Summer means new blood passing through. New faces. And hopefully lots of new boys.

"And let the celebrations start this evening," said Squidge from my left, where he was sitting next to Lia. "All hail, my fellow nutters. As self-appointed King of Rame, this is my decree: Get home. Dispose of thy rucksacks, school bags, etc., etc. Bunging them under the bed where they can gather dust until September is heartily recommended. Wash away all traces of the classroom and be in my back garden for the first barbie of the hols, followed by a DVD. I've got *The Blair Witch Project*—"

"Brill," Mac interrupted. "I've seen it, but I don't mind watching it again. It's a good spooky film about a bunch of kids who stay out in the woods one night and then woohoo*ohooooo* . . . disappear one by one . . ."

"Oh *no*," groaned Lia. "I hate horror films."

"So do I," said Cat. "Becca, you could try out your number for the festival on us instead. Do you know what you're going to sing yet?"

"Not sure. I've been practicing a few different songs, but I might sing one of my own," I replied.

Everyone went quiet for a few moments. I know my mates all think I have a good voice, but they don't rate my songwriting—I know they don't. Maybe in the past I have written some duds, but I'll show them. One day I'll write something totally mind-bogglingly brill.

"Yeah . . . er . . . that would be great," said Cat. "But maybe keep an open mind at this stage, hey? We'd love to hear what you've done though."

"And *then* can we watch *Blair Witch*?" asked Mac.

"Oh noooooo," said Lia. "Let's just listen to Becca sing. So much nicer."

"Don't worry," said Squidge. "I'll hold your hand. It will be great. A bit of nosh, a few songs from our local star singer and then the movie. Heaven. The proprietory—that's me—will be serving sausages, beans, and er . . . sausages and beans. And possibly a burger if you're lucky. And actually it might be my dad who does the barbie, seeing as I am still somewhat out of action, but I shall be there handing the nosh out and you can't ask for more than that."

Squidge had an accident at the beginning of June in which he was knocked off his bike and he hurt his arm and broke his leg. He's going to be okay, but he's still on crutches until the cast comes off his leg.

"I'll bring fizz and crisps," said Cat. "Dad said he'd let me have some from the shop."

Cat's dad runs the local convenience store and sells just about anything and everything. He started off as a grocer and then the post office closed down, so he started selling stamps. And then the flower shop closed, so he started selling a few plants, packets of seeds, and flowers. And then the health shop closed, so he started selling organic and healthy produce. If he hasn't got something, all you have to do is ask for it and it will be on sale a few days later. We tease him, saying that he's slowly taking over the world—building up his empire.

"And I will bring the royal pud," said Lia. "Meena is making one up for us as we speak. Banoffee pie. Yum."

Meena is the Axfords' housekeeper. Lia's dad is Zac Axford, a rich and famous rock star—or at least he was back in the eighties, but he still has a huge following. Their house is awesome. In fact it's not a house—it's called Barton Hall and is so big, it's more like a hotel. The family caused quite a stir when they first arrived in the area a few years ago and I think loads of locals were worried that their peaceful life was to be ruined and that the Axfords would be really annoying and throw wild parties every week with naked girls jumping in swimming pools, drugs, and general "carrying on like maniacs" as Mrs. Edwards from the chippie put it. They're not like that at all. In fact, they're very normal apart from the occasional fab party.

"And I shall bring my gorgeous self," said Mac.

"And Mum promised she'd bake us a double-choc layer cake. My favorite."

Mac is the newcomer to the area. He's been here just over a year and moved down with his mum and his sister, Jade, when his parents split up. They live with his gran and his mum now runs the house as a bed and breakfast. She has fabtastic taste. Very *Elle Decoration*. When they lived in London, she used to be a successful caterer to the rich and famous and she still does a bit of cooking, although, apart from the Axfords, people down here aren't really the sort to have posh private dinner parties. She bakes the most scrumptious cakes in the whole world. I wish my mum was a good cook. I can't remember the last time she baked a cake. I think it was for my ninth birthday. Since then she's bought ready-made ones from the supermarket, which I guess is okay. It's just that sometimes I miss those times when we'd make up the cake mixture together and she'd let me lick the bowl and then put Smarties on the icing.

"I shall bring . . . whatever I can find in the fridge," I said.

And that won't be much, I thought as I envisaged

the contents of our kitchen. Mum's the breadwinner in our family, so lately it's been left to Dad to do the shopping and housework. And it's not exactly something he shows much talent for. Not that he doesn't work—he does. He just doesn't have a proper job or earn much money. He's writing a novel, so I hope it sells and we'll be stonking rich one day, but for the time being, "times is 'ard," as Dad says in a put-on country-yokel voice. He brings in a tiny amount from selling the organic vegetables he grows at the back of our garden, but otherwise all the money that comes in is from Mum's job, which is teaching English as a foreign language over in Plymouth. Dad's idea of shopping and cooking is takeaway with boiled veg from the garden thrown in. The takeaway is one of the things that makes Mum cross, as she says it's expensive. Dad says at least the vegetables don't cost anything. We're forever running out of things like loo paper and lightbulbs—another thing that makes Mum cross, but then she seems to be cross about everything these days. One of my resolutions for the holidays was to go through all the kitchen cupboards, make lists, and help get Dad organized.

Personally I think Mum could have been more helpful in that area, but it was as if she was scoring points against him by letting him fail. They think I don't know they haven't been getting on, but I'm not stupid. Or deaf. I never hear them laughing anymore. And they rarely sit and snuggle up on the sofa the way they used to when we first moved here. Secretly I'm worried that they might be thinking of splitting up. Nothing has been said as far as I know, but I've seen the soaps on telly. I know the signs.

I glanced over at Lia who was laughing with Squidge about something. Sometimes I couldn't help but feel envious of her even though she is one of my best friends. She has it all. She is the most stunning girl I have ever seen. Tall and slim with long white-blond hair and silver-blue eyes. Cat calls Lia and me Rose White and Rose Red because I am also tall but my hair is long and red. Titian red, Mac says. Strawberry blond, I say. Mac says that my hair is my best feature, like silk. I get it from my mum. I think it's probably the only thing we have in common besides the fact that we both live with Dad. I'm much more like Dad in looks as we're both tall and have blue-green eyes and the same wide mouth. Lia's whole family is good-looking. Her mum was a model. Her big sister Star *is* a model in London. Her brother, Ollie, has Zac's dark hair and he's a looker too. And her parents get on so well. I sooo wish mine still did. It worries me a lot, and sometimes lately I don't like going home because of the arguing or, even worse, that awful silence between them that is louder than any angry words. Sometimes I wish I wasn't an only child so I could talk it all over with a brother or sister. I also wish we had a housekeeper like the Axfords do. It would be so brilliant to come home to a cooked supper every night and it might stop some of the stupid rows. . . . Yes, that's it. We need a housekeeper to look after us all. I shall tell Dad as soon as I get home.

"So what's everyone doing tomorrow?" I asked.

Mac pulled a face. "Mum's roped me in for cleaning the rooms we use for bed and breakfast. That crowd are coming down from London."

Cat's face lit up. "Really? Brill. I didn't realize they were coming so soon. TJ and her family aren't arriving until Monday. Can't wait, as we'll get to hang out with them too."

"Oh yeah. Them," I said. Cat hadn't stopped talking about this new crowd for weeks. I don't know why she's so enthusiastic about their group as she's only met one of them so far—a girl called TJ. She was down here from London in the half-term with her mum and dad and she and Cat got talking on the beach. It turned out that, unaware of each other, both of them had been seeing Lia's brother, Ollie. It backfired on poor Ollie, as the girls became friends and he got the old heave-ho. Still, serves him right and I bet he's not that bothered because, being a major cutie, he probably has hundreds of girls falling over him.

Since then, TJ's dad has bought Rose Harbour Cottage near Cremyl to keep as a holiday home, so it looks like they're going to be down here a lot. Cat and TJ have been e-mailing and talking on the phone. I'm not sure how I feel about it as Cat is my friend and, although I have Lia, she's always with Squidge these days and I don't want Cat stolen from me. She seems overly impressed with TJ and can't wait to meet her other mates, Lucy, Izzie, and Nesta.

They're a year older than us and they sound sophisticated. Being from London, they're probably really with it, but I do think that Cat is acting a bit like a kid with a crush. Apparently TJ has long dark hair and Cat's started growing her short, dark hair so that she can look like TJ. Personally, I think a person needs to find her own individual style.

"They're arriving in the morning," said Mac. "The Lovering family. Mr. and Mrs., two boys, and a girl—Lucy. One of the boys is coming with them tomorrow and another coming later."

"And Lucy's already taken," said Cat. "I know exactly what you're thinking, Mac."

"Oh you do, do you? So what am I thinking, Miss Know-It-All?"

"You're thinking: new girl. Wahey."

Mac laughed. "You got me. How did you know?"

"You're transparent."

"No. How do you know that she's *taken*?" Mac asked.

"Oh. TJ told me. Lucy has a thing with Nesta's elder brother. It's a lurve thing. I told you, Mac. It's Izzie who's single."

Mac shrugged his shoulders. "Forgot. I knew it was one of them. Anyway, whatever. As long as one of them is free for the Macster to try his charms out on."

Cat and I rolled our eyes. It's not that Mac isn't fit—he is. So's Squidge for that matter. Girls always check both of them out wherever they go. Squidge is tall and dark and has a lovely open face and Mac is shorter with straw-blond hair and finer features, but he's not the Casanova he likes to think he is. He's too much of a sweetie and I should know, as he was my boyfriend for a while. We called it a day after Easter this year, as both of us felt that we didn't want to be too tied down yet. Since then Mac has fancied himself as a player, but he couldn't be an Ollie Axford if he tried.

As the bus turned the corner, my stop came into view.

"Later," I said as I got up to get off.

There was the most wonderful smell of baking wafting through the house when I opened the front door.

"I'm home," I called.

"In the kitchen, Duchess," Dad called back. When I was little, Dad used to call me Princess, but he changed it to Duchess earlier this year when I entered a nationwide singing competition called Pop Princess. I came in third, so Dad jokes that, as I didn't win the title of princess, it makes me a duchess.

I made my way through and was met by the unexpected sight of Dad wearing a striped blue-and-white apron in a sparkling clean kitchen.

"What's going on?" I asked as I took in the gleaming surfaces and Dad's appearance. Even his hair, which he likes to wear down to his shoulders these days (in an attempt to look rock-starish like Zac Axford, I think) and which he frequently forgets to comb, was looking neat and pushed back from his face.

Dad grinned. "Been doing a bit of housework. I wanted to surprise your mother. And you."

"I'll say," I said as I looked around. There were even fresh flowers on the kitchen table. Pink roses. And he'd set the table for supper.

"Hey, you know that I'm out this evening, don't you?"

Dad pointed at the oven. "End of term barbie at

Squidge's. Yes, I remembered, and that is why, ta-daaa!" He opened the oven with a flourish. "I have baked you some scones to take."

"But Dad . . . I never . . . you can't cook!"

Dad put the baking tray on the cooker top. The scones looked perfect. "No such word as *can't*. I got a recipe, got the ingredients. Bingo. I think they're going to be all right."

I went over and gave him a hug. I really love my dad. And I can see that he is really trying to make things better even if Mum can't.

"I'm sure they will be perfect," I said. "What have you made Mum for supper?"

"All her favorites. Fettucine. Rocket salad from the garden . . ."

I had a sudden moment of panic. "Oh God! It's not her birthday or your anniversary, is it?"

"Hah. We don't need a birthday or anniversary in this house to celebrate. Nope. No . . ." He sat down. "Actually, I have some news. Good news. Things are going to change around here. And for the better, I can tell you."

"Go on, then. Tell me."

Dad grinned like a cheeky kid with a secret. "Can't."

"Why not?"

"I want to wait until Mum's home. I want to tell you both together."

He looked so happy. Happier than I'd seen him in ages.

"You've got a job," I said.

"Noooo. Not that."

I should have known it wasn't that. He'd stopped looking for proper work ages ago after he'd finally got himself a literary agent. It had taken months of rejections before he got accepted by one. First step on the ladder, he'd said at the time. I didn't understand the significance, but he explained that many publishers don't really consider submissions unless they come through an agent. He was over the moon with the news, but then most of the year went by and his agent still hadn't managed to sell his book, even though she'd sent it out loads of times to different editors. His rejection file grew fatter. That's when the arguments between Mum and Dad began to get worse and more frequent. They were mostly about money. She wanted him to get a part-time job.

He wanted to follow his dream or at least give it a chance. He'd started work on a new idea and was really excited about it and had sent the outline and first three chapters off just over a week ago.

"It's your new book," I said. "It is, isn't it? Your agent's got you a deal."

Dad couldn't keep it in any longer and his face split into a beam. "Okay. You guessed. Oh, what the hell, I'll tell you. It's hours until your mother gets back. Yes. The agent phoned this morning. Actually she phoned last week, but I didn't want to say anything until it was definite, as these things can always collapse at the last moment. But the news is good. Not one but two publishers wanted my book. They went to auction over it."

"Auction? What does that mean?"

"It means, my little Duchess, that they try to outbid each other. It means the advance they're willing to pay gets pushed higher and higher."

"And . . ."

Dad began to dance round the kitchen. "*We're in the money*," he sang. "*We're in the money*."

2   Truth, Dare, Kiss, or Promise

I WOKE THE NEXT MORNING with a start. There was a noise outside the tent. Voices. Someone was out there. . . .

I snuggled down further into my sleeping bag, my heart pounding madly, and strained to listen. Then I realized. Stupid me! I wasn't in a sleeping bag. I wasn't in a tent. I was at home. In my bed. Completely safe. Phew, what a relief, I thought as I pushed the duvet off. I'd been dreaming that I was lost in the woods like in *The Blair Witch Project*. What a horrible film that had been. Really scary. Not like some horror films which are so over the top with special effects that you can have a laugh about them, this one had seemed real and left a lot to the imagination. Mine had gone into overdrive and I'd got really spooked. So had Lia. I could see that she had been freaked out by it too and was glad when the lights came back on at the end.

I could still hear voices, though. Raised voices in the kitchen below. I got out of bed, crept out on to the landing, then down a few stairs and strained to listen.

"I really don't think that's a good idea," I heard Mum say.

"Oh come on, love," said Dad. "Things like this don't happen every day. One should celebrate the good times. They don't always last long. Heaven knows it's going to be a hard slog from now on, when I actually have to get on with finishing the book."

I hovered for a moment in case they were about to launch into one of their rows.

"I know," said Mum, "and I think it is great news. I said so last night, but why can't we have a *small* celebration? Something that doesn't cost too much."

I hopped down the remaining stairs and went to join them in the kitchen. "Celebration? What celebration?"

Dad, back in disheveled mode with his hair in its usual unkempt fashion, was wearing his navy fleece dressing gown and sitting at the table. Mum, dressed in her work clothes—navy suit, white shirt, hair tied back neatly in a clip—was at the sink.

"Morning, love," said Dad and pointed at the kettle. "Tea?"

I shook my head and went to the fridge. "I'll have some juice, thanks. So what's going on?"

"I think we should mark the occasion of my first book deal," said Dad. "And I think we should go somewhere fabulous to do it."

"Great idea," I said as I sat at the table. "Where?"

Mum continued washing up at the sink. She turned round and sighed. "I don't see why we can't just go to a nice restaurant over in Plymouth or to the View Café up at Whitsand."

"What were you thinking, Dad?"

Dad gazed dreamily out of the window. "Somewhere further afield," he said. "Seeing as we haven't been away for a while as a family, I thought maybe a city break. Paris, London, Barcelona, Prague, Istanbul . . . What do you think?"

"Wow. Yes to all the above," I said. Usually it was the Axfords who were jetting off somewhere fab and although they did take Cat and me along when they were celebrating Lia's mum's birthday in Morocco, it would be great to go away with my own mum and dad for a change.

Mum leaned back against the kitchen counter and crossed her arms. "You're not earning J. K. Rowling amounts of money, you know."

"But he did get a good deal, didn't you, Dad? Didn't you tell her that the book went to auction?"

Dad nodded.

"And didn't you tell Becca that the advance is only enough money to last a year?" said Mum. "And we have debts to pay off from earlier this year, credit cards, overdraft, not to mention the mortgage. I'm only being practical. And don't forget that your agent will take her ten percent, and we don't get all the money at once. See, Becca, the advance that the publisher gives gets split into three amounts. One lot on signature of contract. A second on acceptance of the book once it's written, and the third on publication."

"Yeah. And then the book goes into the shops and we'll be rich. Hurrah," I said.

"Not necessarily," said Mum. "Who knows if a

book is going to sell or not? We won't know until it's out there. And who knows even if the final manuscript will be accepted? We can't go frittering money away that isn't even in the bank yet."

I could see by Dad's shoulders that she'd put a complete dampener on his good news. She always did this lately. It wasn't fair. I was with Dad on this. Celebrate the good times. Rock and roll.

"I think we should go," I said. "Seize the day and all that."

Dad smiled weakly. "Well, it's up to your mother really."

Mum groaned and banged down a cup she'd been washing on to the draining board. "Oh for *heaven's* sake. Why is it always *me* who has to be the sensible one? The responsible grown-up? Why do I have to be the one who counts the pennies? Well, you know what? I won't do it this time. Go on. Spend your money. Book a trip away. Just don't blame me if further down the line you regret not putting the money away."

I'm out of here, I thought. I hated seeing Dad look so unhappy, especially when for once he really did have good news and was only trying to share it.

"You're such a killjoy," I blurted to Mum. "We never have any fun in this house any more."

I got up and went out the back door. I didn't want to be there. I'd get breakfast somewhere else. Somewhere where there wasn't a strained atmosphere or people rowing.

And I didn't want to go on any trip if this is how Mum was going to be. Why couldn't she for once try and be like the old Mum she used to be, who was fun and up for anything?

"If I were a character from fiction, who would I be?" asked Squidge as he lay back on Cawsand beach.

We were silent while we thought about it. We being Mac, Lia, Cat, Squidge, and I. We were lying in the sun in a line on beach towels supplied by Squidge's mum. We'd been there most of the day just hanging out, paddling a bit, talking, reading books and mags, and having a laugh. I loved being down on the beach with my mates and was almost feeling happy again as I breathed in the seaside smell of seaweed, salty air, and suntan lotion.

"Dickon from that book, *The Secret Garden*," I said.

"Perfect," said Cat.

"No way," said Squidge as he sat up, whipped out a pair of dark glasses, and put them on. "That's such an old-fashioned book. No. Look at me. I'm loads hipper than that. I reckon Keanu Reeves in *The Matrix*."

"Dream on, babe," I said. "I chose Dickon because of his personality rather than his looks. Although he's got an open face like you, he's also a nature boy and loves roaming about outdoors. And anyway, *The Matrix* is almost as old now as *The Secret Garden*."

"Tosh," said Mac. "You're talking out your bum."

Cat burst out laughing. "Now that I would like to see. Can you imagine? Be a great trick to do at parties."

"*The Matrix* will always be cool," said Squidge and he lay back down again. He looked miffed that I'd compared him to a character from an old novel, but it was his idea that we play this stupid "If I Were a Character from Fiction" game.

"What about me?" asked Mac. "Bond? 007?"

Cat, Lia, and I spluttered with laughter, causing Mac to look at us with a hurt expression.

"Give us a break," said Cat. "All the Bonds have been tall. And you, my fine furry friend, are, er . . ."

"Vertically challenged," I said, laughing. "Which is a politically correct way of saying short."

"No way am I short," Mac objected. "I'm five foot six. Medium."

"And very cute," said Lia.

Squidge thumped her playfully on the arm.

"Hey! And so are you," she said and rolled her eyes. "Honestly! Boys."

Mac looked put out. "Looks don't tell you everything about a man," he said sulkily. "I have an inner James Bond."

"And I have an inner Keanu Reeves," said Squidge, who was quick as always to support his mate.

"Okay, so I'm not James Bond," said Mac. "Who then?"

"Tintin," said Cat.

Mac almost choked. "He has red hair. You're not taking this seriously."

"Am," said Cat.

"Okay, then you're Betty Boop."

"Am not."

"Are," said Mac. "Cute with dark hair. Very Betty Boop."

"Betty Boop? But she's a cartoon," said Cat. "I'm a human being!"

"Oh, stop arguing," I yelled up into the sky. "Why is everyone always arguing these days?"

Mac put his hand on my arm. "We're not arguing. We're joshing. Big difference."

"Okay. So who am I, then?" I asked.

Mac scrutinized me. "Easy. The Lady of Shalott. I always reckoned you look like one of those girls in the Pre-Raphaelite paintings with your long, red, silk hair and pale skin. The ones by Edward Burne-Jones, not Rossetti—his ladies were dark with big full mouths. Your features are more delicate."

"Delicate? Sounds deadly dull," I said. "Weren't the Pre-Raphaelite women all tragic heroines?"

"I guess," said Squidge. "Yeah. All mourning their knight-type boyfriends who had gone off on crusades or were doing other brave deeds."

Cat sat up and looked wistfully out to sea. "Shame we don't get knights on white horses anymore," she said. "I think I'd like all that. It would be so romantic being rescued by one and then carried off to a castle somewhere. All we get now are oiks on bicycles who want to show off by riding with no hands and then usually fall off. So actually, I reckon our life now is far more tragic that it was for those heroines back then. There's nothing more tragic than a lack of local talent."

"I agree. I am a modern-day tragic heroine," I said and sat up and put on my best noble-but-tragic look. "I think I might write a song about it, in fact." I strained to think of the right words for a song about heroines, but all that would come was: Lady Bec, what a wreck, give us a peck, oh Lady Bec. God. Rubbish, I thought.

"Pff," said Mac. "What's tragic about your life?"

"Everything," I said. "You don't know."

"Rubbish," he said. "From what I heard you had a great time with one of Ollie's mates in Morocco."

I tossed my hair back. "Henry. That was a holiday romance. And anyway he lives in London. He e-mails sometimes, but I don't do long-distance love."

Cat looked awkward. "Oh yeah," she said. "Your song."

She was referring to the song I had sung for them last night after supper at Squidge's. I had written it about Henry and the title was "Long-distance Love is Just Too Long for Me." It hadn't gone down well. I could tell by everyone's faces. "*Long-distance love, long-distance love, long-distant love, it stinks,*" I'd sung. They'd tried to be enthusiastic, but I know them all well enough to know when they are faking it and it wasn't my best song—even I knew that. When I sang another song afterward, a soul number from the sixties, they were genuinely impressed and applauded like mad.

"Why not stay in touch with Henry? You got along so well," said Lia. "And Cat's stayed in touch with Jamie, haven't you, Cat?"

Cat nodded as I flicked my hair back again. "So?" I said. "It won't last. Love never does. And anyway, I'm through with boys. And I'm through with relationships."

"Since when?" said Cat.

"Since now. I've just decided." Since my parents started arguing, I thought—but I wasn't going to say that to my mates. I didn't want it to get around the area that they weren't getting on. I was still hoping that they might get over it and we could go back to being the happy family that we once were.

"Yeah right," said Mac.

"No really. You don't know me. I really, really am through with boys. Relationships stink."

"No they don't," said Lia. "Sometimes they can be great."

"Well, you and Squidge are the exception," I said. "And you are still in what the magazines call the honeymoon stage. Just you wait. It won't last. It never does."

"*Becca*," Cat objected. "Why so cynical all of a sudden? You're usually the most romantic of all of us."

"I'm just being practical," I said and then realized that I sounded like my mum and felt cross. "Oh shut up."

"You shut up, misery guts," said Squidge. "We're not having this, are we, guys? Truth, dare, kiss, or promise. Only you don't get to choose. It's kiss. I, as King of Rame, and my royal subjects all decree that you shall get back on the horse immediately. . . ."

"What blooming horse? Horses, knights—you

lot don't half talk some rubbish. And anyway, you ride a bike not a horse—or at least you did until you broke your leg."

"I am speaking metaphorically. The horse of life. Of love. Of relationships," said Squidge.

"Oo-er," chorused the rest of us.

"Get him and his big words," said Cat. "But I agree. Kiss. You must . . . you must . . ."

"Kiss the next boy who comes onto the beach," Squidge finished for her.

"No way," I said. "It will be some local nerd with spots and bandy legs."

"Too late to object," said Mac. "Come on, guys. Let's go and wait at the benches by the café and see who comes along."

Mac, Cat, and Lia got up and helped Squidge to his feet and onto his crutches. Then they gathered their belongings and stood over me. Squidge even waved a crutch at me.

"Shan't," I said. "And you can't make me."

"Cowardy, cowardy custard," said Mac. "You're scared, aren't you? It's not cynicism. It's fear."

"Don't be pathetic. No way I'm scared."

"So do it," said Cat.

I stood up and followed the others to the bench by the alleyway that led from Cawsand Square down to the beach. I got out my lip gloss and applied some. Got out my brush and brushed my hair.

"I'll show you who's scared or not," I said. "Bring them on."

"Prepare to pucker," Mac said to no one in particular as we took up our places to wait.

First a family of three came by. A dad, a mum, and a baby in a pram. I got up to approach the man.

Squidge pulled me back. "*Nooooo*. Er . . . there are rules. No married men. No men over . . . thirty, and none under, er . . . thirteen."

"Fine," I said and sat back down.

Mr. and Mrs. McKeever were next. He's at least seventy, so he was out.

After them was a bunch of girls who looked about twelve. They glanced flirtily at Mac and Squidge. Lia immediately linked arms with Squidge while Mac gave them his best cool look, which makes him look like he's about to fall asleep any second.

And then no one for about ten minutes.

"This is hopeless," I said. "Let's go somewhere else."

"No wait," said Squidge. "There are some people getting out of a car in the square. Look."

We peered down the alleyway and could see that a very bright turquoise car had just parked outside the pub. Not locals, I thought. I would have remembered that car. A balding man who looked as though he was in his forties got out, followed by a very pretty girl with shoulder-length blond hair. She was wearing a really cool outfit. A wraparound flowery dress that looked vintage over a pair of jeans and the most outrageous high wedge sandals with a big red flower on them. Definitely not local.

A moment later, a lady with long blond hair in a plait got out the back. Must be the mum, I thought. In contrast to the girl, who looked really stylish, the mum looked as if she'd thrown her clothes on in the dark. She had a red-and-white striped T-shirt on over a floral lime-green and orange skirt. Not a good combination.

Suddenly Cat nudged me. "Now, this could be interesting," she said as a boy who looked about fifteen or sixteen got out of the back.

Hmm. Not half bad, I thought. He was medium

height, medium build and dressed in jeans, T-shirt, and baseball cap. He wasn't drop-dead gorgeous like Lia's brother, but he was cute. It would be no hardship at all to snog him.

"No," I said. "They might be boyfriend and girl-friend."

"Don't think so," said Mac, who was ogling the girl like he'd never seen one before. "They have the same eyes. I think they're brother and sister."

"Yeah," said Squidge. "And the baldie man looks like the dad and the one with the plait looks like the mum."

"Watch out. They're coming this way," said Lia as the four newcomers spotted the alley and the ocean beyond, then began to make their way toward us.

Cat, Mac, Lia, and Squidge looked at the man, the woman, and the girl as they walked past, then turned to watch the boy, who was slouching behind. As he approached, they turned to look at me to see if I was going to cop out or cop off.

I took a deep breath, slipped off the wall, walked up to the boy, and caught his arm as he passed. He turned to face me.

"Er, excuse me a moment," I said and before I could chicken out, I leaned in and kissed him.

"Wha . . . spluh . . . wuh," spluttered the boy.

He took a step back and looked me up and down, then his face split into a wide smile. "Wow," he said. "I think I'm going to like Cornwall."

Holy Crapoly

I DIDN'T GIVE THE BOY a chance to say anything else, because when I glanced over at his parents and saw the look on their faces, I decided that I'd better leg it. They didn't look too happy about their son being accosted by a stranger the moment he'd got out of the car. The girl, on the other hand, cracked up laughing.

"Way to go, bro. Seems like it's your lucky day," I heard her say as I turned and fled the scene, leaving the boy standing there looking bewildered.

Lia, Mac and Cat had the same idea and with Squidge limping behind on his crutches, we ran up the alley laughing our heads off, then down one of the back streets, away from the square.

"Thank God they're not local," I said as I peeped round a corner and looked back at the brightly colored car they had arrived in. "Hopefully that's the last we'll see of them."

"I don't know," said Cat. "He looked nice. And he didn't seem to mind being snogged, after the initial shock."

It was true. He was quite appealing with his twinkly blue eyes, but I shrugged the experience off. It had only been a game. He was probably passing through with his family like so many others at this time of year, on their way further into Cornwall to resorts like Penzance or Padstow. What did I care? I was through with boys.

"Lia and I are heading back to my place," said Squidge when we got close to the cottage where he lived. "Want to come in?"

Mac shook his head. "I'll just come and collect my bike."

"Me too," I said.

"Cat?" asked Squidge.

Cat shook her head and looked at her watch. "No. I promised I'd babysit Emily as Dad and Jen are going off to look at the new house again."

"How's that all going?" asked Mac.

We all knew that moving house meant a lot to Cat. It meant her own room for the first time in her life. At the moment, she was still having to share with Emily, who was only six and, although cute, sometimes drove Cat mad.

"I can't wait," said Cat. "If all goes according to plan, they exchange next week and then we should be set to move at the beginning of August. Hurrah!"

"Why can't Luke or Joe look after Emily for a change?" I asked. "It's always you. I reckon your brothers get off easily." I felt for Cat sometimes. Since her mum died when she was nine, she's had to be almost a replacement mum. She does more than the rest of us in the way of household chores and cooking, and she has to look after her younger brothers and sister. August is going to be a big month for her because her dad is going to remarry, which we all think is fab—not only because his fiancée, Jen, is really nice, but also because it may mean that at last Cat will have more freedom. I hope so.

Cat laughed. "Nice idea and you're right, but can you imagine if we left them to babysit? Last time we left Luke in charge, he and Joe decided to pretend that they were Daleks from *Dr. Who*. Joe got a pan jammed on his head and Luke had the loo plunger stuck to his forehead and they both had to be taken to the ER. They're walking disasters. So nah, not an option yet. Be easier when Jen moves in with us properly. See yas."

She took off up the road and we followed Squidge and Lia toward his house.

"Want to come back to mine?" asked Mac. "Mum will probably do us a snack or something if you're hungry."

I nodded. I didn't want to go home yet even though there was a text from both Dad and Mum on my phone—the one from Dad asking if I was okay and did I want to go for ice cream over at Whitsand, and the one from Mum telling me to SWITCH my phone ON. (I had switched it on to check for messages, then switched it off again.) I didn't want to talk to her yet. I felt cross with her for ruining everything. What was there to go home for? It was the summer holidays. What did they expect me to do? Sit there and referee their fights? Or act happy families as if nothing had happened and it was all just hunky-dory? No way.

"So what's going on?" asked Mac after we'd said

good-bye to the others and got our bikes from the back of Squidge's cottage.

"Nothing. Why?" I replied as we headed off up the hill.

"Because I know you, Rebecca Howard, and you aren't your usual self."

"I'm all right. I did what Squidge asked and kissed that boy, didn't I?"

"Yeah but . . . you don't seem very happy."

"Am."

"Aren't."

"Am."

Mac slowed his bike down and motioned for me to do the same. He put his hand on my arm. "Listen. If you don't want to talk, I understand, but if you do, I'm here, okay?"

He was looking at me so kindly that I felt tears prick my eyes. I tried to sniff them away.

"See," said Mac. "I *knew* there was something."

"Just leave it, will you? Don't be nice to me. I hate it when people are nice to me." I felt my tears turning to anger. What is the matter with me lately? I thought. Part of me feels like I want to scream.

Another part wants to kick something. Another part wants to blub like a baby. Best push it all down. It freaked me out to think about what might happen if Mum and Dad really did break up. Mac's mum and dad split up and his dad lives up in London and he hardly ever sees him. I couldn't bear to not see my mum and dad, so if I don't think about it, it might not happen. "Just leave me alone, *okay*?"

I said "okay" a tad aggressively and Mac looked hurt.

"Okay," he said and got back on his bike and cycled away fast.

I felt rotten. He was only trying to be kind. God, I'm acting like my mother, I realized. Pushing people away when they're trying to be nice. No way do I want to be like her.

I cycled after him as fast as I could, but couldn't catch him up.

He got back to his house about five minutes before me. As I cycled into the courtyard in front of his gran's house, I saw him disappearing through the rose arch that led into their back garden.

I quickly got off my bike and ran after him.

"I'm sorry," I said as he was about to go in the back door.

He shrugged, but I could see that he was still miffed with me.

"Look. Bad day. If you really want to know what's going on then I'll tell you. It's . . . stuff at home. Mum and . . ." I felt the tears prickling again.

Mac immediately melted. He came and put his arm round me and led me to the picnic table at the back of the garden. "Come on, you idiot," he said.

We sat at the table and I stared at the grass willing the tears to go away.

"Your folks not getting on?" asked Mac.

I shook my head, then nodded. "I'm really, *really* worried that it's serious this time. They've had rows before, but this is different. They used to make up before. And if they do break up . . . what will happen to us? Where will we live? *How* will we live? What will happen to me?" A huge sob threatened to escape from my throat and I tried to swallow it back down.

Mac squeezed my hand. "Well, if anyone understands about that, it's me. I remember when we lived in London and my mum and dad weren't getting on, I hated it too."

I nodded again. "I . . . I can't stand being there anymore. I . . . you know what, Mac? I don't even like going home to my own house. I always try and think of excuses to stay out so that I don't have to face them. It's horrible sometimes, like when you guys have all gone home for supper, I stay out and go places on my own—and last week I was sitting on one of the benches at the top of Kingsand Beach and Mr. O'Riley walked past and asked if I had a home to go to. I know he was joking, but I thought, actually no, I don't. Not one I feel at home in anymore . . ."

Mac looked at me with a mixture of sympathy and panic. "I'm so sorry, Bec. . . ."

And then the floodgates opened and I started bawling.

Mac looked round as if he was worried that someone might be watching or listening and think that he'd said something to upset me.

"Oh God, Becca, don't cry," he said as he squeezed my hand again. "I hate it when you cry."

He squeezed my hand really hard.

"*Ow!*" I cried. "YOU asked me what was WRONG. *YOU* started it."

Mac looked at a total loss as to what to do and just stared at me as tears dripped down my cheeks. I didn't care. In a strange way, it was a relief to cry it out.

Mac took his hand away and stood up. "Well, I'm sorry," he said and he began pacing up and down, looking around, then looking at me in dismay as if he didn't know what to do next. He sat down then got up again and started pacing again. "Oh, *fromage*. Um. What to do? Um . . . cup of tea? What would you like? We can sort this out, Becca, if you just stop crying."

The sight of him flapping about like he had ants in his pants suddenly struck me as funny and I stopped crying and started laughing. This caused Mac to look more bewildered than ever.

"Oh God. Why are you laughing?" he asked, then sighed and sat back down opposite me. "Crumbling crustaceans. Girls. I'll never understand them. Do you want me to get Cat?"

I shook my head and tried to make myself calm down by breathing slowly.

"I tell you what," said Mac. "We need a plan. Yes. That's what we need. A plan to cheer you up. What can we do?"

"We can get my mum to stop acting like a total misery-guts and be NICE to my dad for a change. He doesn't deserve the way she treats him. I really HATE her sometimes."

Mac looked even more taken aback as I really shouted the word *hate* loudly. "Ohhh right," he said, looking more confused than ever. "Yes. That's it. Yes. Good. Cry. Laugh. Shout. Yes. Let it all out. Oh God . . ."

He looked like he wanted me to do anything *but* let it all out, but I decided to take his advice. I'd read in one of my girlie magazines that one of the best ways to de-stress is by letting it all out.

I got up and went to the nearest tree and began to kick it. "I HATE HER," I shouted at the top of my voice, then, just for good measure, gave the tree a few more kicks.

There was a silence. Then I heard someone cough.

"Hey! What did that poor tree do to you?" said a boy's voice.

"Ohmigod! Who is that?" I called. "Who's there? Mac! Quick—there's a prowler in the garden. There! Behind that bush!"

There was a rustle and then a boy appeared. A *familiar* boy, the one I'd snogged down on the beach and he looked like he was having a hard time not laughing.

He held out his hand. "Hi. Seeing as we have done the face-suckee thing, maybe I should introduce myself. I'm Laurence Lovering, but my mates call me Lal. I'm not a prowler. I'm a guest here. My family are staying here for two weeks. We just arrived. The lady back at the house up there told me to look at the garden while she made some tea."

"Er, that's my mum," said Mac, getting up from the table. "Hi. I'm Mac. My mum runs the place."

A moment later, the blonde girl from the beach appeared besides Lal. "Hi," she said. "I'm Lucy."

Holy crapoly, it's that mob from London, I thought. And oh *no*, I must look a right mess with swollen eyes and I bet my mascara's run too.

Lal and Lucy looked at Mac, then at me.

"Oh yes. Me. Um. I am . . . Becca. Yes. I don't

normally go round kicking trees and snogging strange boys, you know. . . ."

"Don't tell me that you snog trees and kick boys," said Lal and Mac and Lucy laughed.

I gave Lal a filthy look.

"Sorry," said Lal with a big grin. "I interrupted. You were saying?"

"I was saying—or at least *trying* to say—that I am quite normal, really. Honestly, I am. Not mad at all."

"Shame," said Lal, "because I like mad girls. They make life interesting."

And then he held eye contact for a few moments and I felt my stomach do that leapy-lurch thing that it does when there is fanciability in the air. Hmmm, I thought. Maybe I'm not quite through with boys just yet. . . .

Revenge

"I DON'T WANT TO GO. Sorry," I said when Mum showed me a holiday brochure on Tuesday evening over supper.

Mum took a long breath. One of those breaths that tells you that someone is having a hard time restraining themselves from socking someone else in the face. That someone else being me. I didn't care. She'd ruined enough good times lately.

"What do you mean you don't want to go?" she asked. "You were all for it last week when your dad first suggested it."

"Changed my mind."

"Oh, Becca. You can be so difficult sometimes," she said with a sigh.

"Me, difficult? It was you who didn't want to go anywhere. You wanted to go to a restaurant in Plymouth. Remember?"

For a moment Mum looked weary. "I suppose. Yes, I suppose I changed my mind too."

"Well, now I think a restaurant is a good idea too."

Dad came in from the garden, where he'd been to collect some basil leaves. "So what's with the long face, Duchess?" he asked as he tore the leaves up, sprinkled them over our pasta, and turned to Mum. "What's going on? Have you told her the news?"

Mum shrugged. "She doesn't want to go."

Dad looked taken aback. "Doesn't want to go to Prague? Are you kidding? It's supposed to be one of the most beautiful cities in Europe."

"I think Mum was right last week," I said as I pushed my food around my plate. "I think that we should all be sensible and you should save your money, Dad. I mean, we live in such a fantastic holiday place—why leave it?"

"Because your dad has just booked—" Mum started.

"Er . . . this not wanting to go," Dad interrupted, "it wouldn't have anything to do with a certain boy who has been phoning here over the last few days, would it?"

"No," I replied as I pushed my plate away. "What boy?"

Actually, it had everything to do with "a certain boy." Lal Lovering. He was a total godsend and had been just what I needed to take my mind off my problems, i.e. Mum and Dad.

Since Saturday, we'd hung out every day and I'd taken him round all the good sites I know. The weather had been sunny and it was great to show someone new around as I got to see the area through his eyes and was reminded how fab it is. Plus, being with him gave me an excuse to avoid my Cornish mates. Not because I don't like them, but because, being such close mates, they'd have picked up on the fact that I wasn't my normal self and asked questions like Mac had the other day and I didn't want that. It brought too many feelings up that I didn't know how to deal with. They were just happy that I'd got together with Lal—Squidge in particular. He reckoned that he was totally responsible for his first love match and told me to call him Cupid. Lal didn't know me as well as they did so wouldn't know if I was subdued or not saying what was on my mind.

On Sunday, we explored the villages and bays over in Kingsand and Cawsand and I showed him the secret beach out at Penlee Point that only the locals know about. It's perfect for kissing and cuddling and not being seen and he seemed well up for a lot of that. In fact that was one of the things I liked about him. We did a bit of the usual finding out about each other: fave movies, music, what star sign, and so on, and I discovered that although he's a bit flash and full of himself, underneath he's a nice guy who simply wants to have a good time. Mainly what he liked doing was snogging, playing with my hair, and holding hands. And that suited me perfectly for the time being. Normally I like to talk about everything. About what's going on in my head. All sorts of things, but not lately. I'd rather have a boy who could distract me from what was happening in my head than one who wants to talk, talk, talk, and Lal certainly wasn't a boy who was big on communication. He was into action. Demonstration. It felt great to be wanted so much. No games. No trying to be cool.

Lal was easily the most affectionate boyfriend I've ever had. In fact, he reminded me of an overexcited puppy, desperate for attention, but so cute that you didn't mind giving him a cuddle. He made a refreshing change from some of the boys I'd been out with, who had either been too shy or fearful of rejection to say what they really wanted. Lal had no inhibitions. He knew what he wanted all right, and that was to get as up close and personal as he possibly could as often as he could. I had to fight him off from going too far, as he got fresh down on the beach and put his hands inside my T-shirt. I soon slapped his hands away as I didn't know him that well. He was okay about it, though, and said I couldn't blame him for trying. He said that any boy in his right mind would try. He makes me feel like I am the most desirable girl on the planet and that's why he can't keep his hands off me.

First thing on Monday, we did the Whitsand side of the peninsula. We started out at the View Café at the top of the cliff, where I almost had to drag one of the waitresses off him. Her name's Shazza and she's blonde with big boobs that she has no inhibitions about showing off. Lal's eyes were out on stalks when she leaned over our table to pass him the menu. She's actually really nice and a laugh, but she's such a flirt when boys are around. She's one of those girls who doesn't have many female friends because she prefers the company of boys. Squidge calls her HHH—Hot Hormones on Heels. I'd gone off to the ladies' for a moment and when I came back, she'd almost wrapped herself round Lal. I soon saw her off, but I could see that Lal was well flattered and, if I was honest, it was cool to know that the boy I was with was on the Cornish Wanted List because he was so fanciable.

After juice at the café and a long snog to make sure that Shazza got the picture, we climbed down the cliff path to join Lia, Squidge, Cat, and Mac to go swimming on one of the more remote beaches at Whitsand (which is where Lal tried to get inside my T-shirt when he thought the others weren't looking). Later, we walked through the waves in our bare feet, holding hands, and I felt like I was in a romantic movie. That is, until he picked me up and threatened to throw me into the sea with all my clothes on. But even that felt romantic—although I have a sneaking suspicion that what he really wanted was to see what I looked like in a wet T-shirt. He's that kind of boy. Walking testosterone,

Cat would say. Come to think of it, he and Shazza would probably make the perfect couple. I don't mind Lal being a Randy Andy, though, because he soon stops the funny business if I say "NoooooOO." And if that didn't ever work, I could always try my backup method, which is a quick knee in the goolies. I reckon that should work if a boy gets overexcited. Luckily I haven't had to do it to anyone yet.

This morning, we got up really early and went up to Squidge's favorite place to watch the sunrise. It's a ruined church on top of a hill out at Rame Head and the view from there is spectacular. Sea, sky, and miles and miles of unspoiled coastline. It's stunning at the best of times, but so early in the morning it was amazingly peaceful, like the whole world was sleeping except for Lal and me. We sat for ages snuggled up in our fleeces, him behind me and me leaning back between his knees.

I was looking forward to spending the rest of his holiday with him. I had a whole itinerary mapped out. The last thing I needed was to be dragged away on some history tour of a strange foreign city. Urgy lurgies. No thanks.

"That boy from London who keeps calling," said Mum. "Lal, isn't it?"

I shrugged my shoulders. I didn't want to discuss it with them. He was my secret. My escape. My proof to myself that it was possible to have a good fun relationship. "I'm just showing him around," I said. "As a favor."

"Favor to whom?" asked Mum. "Don't his family mind? I'd have thought they would want to spend time with him, seeing as it's their family holiday."

I shrugged. "No one's objected so far. Cat's been showing his sister, Lucy, round, and his mum and dad like going for long walks. So everyone's happy. Anyway, some of their other friends arrived yesterday and more are coming next week."

"Oh yes, I heard. The people who bought Rose Cottage. The doctors?" asked Mum.

I nodded. "Yeah. And their daughter, TJ, and a couple of her friends."

I knew all about them from Lal and also from Cat, who didn't seem to able to talk about anyone else these days.

Dad sat down and looked at me pleadingly.

"You'll love Prague, Bec, so no more of this nonsense about not wanting to go. And we are still being sensible. I went into a travel agent's yesterday to see what was on offer and he had a fantastic deal going. A last-minute thing, so we're going to be staying at one of the best hotels for next to nothing and the flights are all included. Can't go wrong."

"How long for?" I asked.

"Friday to Monday. We leave this Friday. Luckily there's a direct flight from Bristol, so we just have to get there and off we go. Back Monday."

"*This* Friday?" I asked.

Dad nodded. "Think you can bear to be parted from loverboy for that long?"

"Loverboy?" asked Mum. "She's only just met him! Of course she can bear to be parted."

"It's not that," I said. "I have to practice for the Maker Festival. I have to sing every day to keep my voice at its peak." It was partly true. It was something that I had learned when I entered the Pop Princess competition. The singing coaches had made us practice and *practice*, vocal exercise after vocal exercise. And it worked. If I did the exercises regularly, my range was much wider and I could sing with more ease than if I neglected to do them.

"You can sing anywhere," said Dad. "You can sing in your hotel room."

"I guess."

I tried persuading them that a weekend away alone was what they needed, but they weren't having that for a moment.

"We wouldn't dream of leaving you by yourself," said Dad in horror. "And anyway, this is a treat to be shared by all of us."

I tried asking them to put it off until the end of the summer hols (when Lal and his family would have gone).

"Can't do later," said Mum. "It's booked and I have leave to take right now, which is why it's all worked out so perfectly."

I tried telling them that I secretly had a condition that makes your blood clot on long plane journeys and that it would be dangerous to travel. I explained that I hadn't told them about it before because I didn't want to worry them.

And then they started laughing.

I could see that I wasn't going to win and Dad was being so enthusiastic that I felt I couldn't spoil things by being too difficult. It wouldn't be fair on him.

So that was that. My fate was decided. Snatched from the good times just as they were starting to get interesting.

Sometimes life can be *oh* so cruel.

5   Prague

"IT'S GOING TO BE AWFUL being away from you," I told Lal when we came up from our good-bye snogathon on Friday morning. He'd been such a sweetie and had turned up not long after breakfast with a gorgeous bunch of roses. The sensible part of me thought, What a stupid prezzie, seeing as I'm going to be away for three days. They will probably be dead by the time I get back. But another part was touched. I'm a sucker for flowers.

"Just try to enjoy yourself," said Lal wistfully as we sat on the wall outside my house where we were screened from my nosy parents by a large rhododendron bush. "Do it for me. I couldn't bear to think of you being unhappy."

"I'll try," I said, and attempted to look brave. "But it's going to be hard. And I guess I'd better go in now and finish packing. Although I don't really care what I take or what I look like because you're not going to be with me." .

Lal nodded and stared sadly at his feet. "Ditto."

"Bye then," I sighed.

"Bye," he sighed.

He stood up, gave me a last lingering look, then turned and walked away. I felt so miserable. And so did he. I could tell by his slumped shoulders.

I couldn't stand it. Three whole days without him.

"Laa*aaal*," I called.

He turned and we ran into each other's arm for a final, *final* snog. Soooo romantic, in a chick-flick kind of way. Then he kissed my forehead, turned, and slouched off again. And he really did go this time.

Down the road. Round the corner.

I waited for five minutes for him to come back again for another passionate parting. But he didn't. Huh . . . oh well.

I think it was in *Romeo and Juliet* that there was that line: "Parting is such sweet sorrow." It was sad, yeah, but also quite enjoyable in a weird way. Better than feeling nothing.

• • •

On the car journey to Bristol, Lal and I texted back and forth about how bad we felt, but after that, although I tried my best, it was hard to stay feeling tragic for long. I love traveling and the hustle and bustle of getting to the airport, doing the shops in the departure area, trying on sunglasses, sampling all the perfumes, boarding the plane, and flying off into the clouds. It took my mind off Lal and the pain of being separated from him.

As the plane began its descent into Prague, I looked over at Dad and gave him a big smile. It was only for a weekend, and even Mum was making an effort to be in a good mood.

The weather was warm and our hotel was utterly, butterly fab. I knew I was going to love it there the moment we stepped into the vast, marble-floored reception area. It was well posh, with ginormous vases full of white lilies that smelled heavenly.

"Five stars," Mum said with a grin and gave me a wink.

After we checked in, the man at reception asked if we'd like to eat there that evening and invited us to take a look at the dining room. It was spectacular.

Wood-paneled walls, linen tablecloths, and more flowers—orchids on each table and, in the center of the room, a huge, round glass vase stuffed with about fifty white orchids. They must have cost a fortune. It looked so sophisticated and so did the people sitting there. Not like Cornish tourists dressed in T-shirts, shorts, and flip-flops. These people were dressed in their best going-out clothes and it was only four o'clock in the afternoon. I was glad that despite what I'd said to Lal about not caring what I looked like, I had actually packed some decent clothes.

We went out onto the terrace at the back to take in the view. The hotel was on the river and to our right, we could see an old gray stone bridge lined with statues. Behind that, in the distance on a hill, stood a castle that looked like it was straight out of a Disney movie, with turrets reaching up to the sky.

"That's the famous Charles Bridge," said Dad, pointing toward the bridge, "and beyond that is Prague Castle."

It looked wonderful—so old and yet still standing. The trip was getting better by the hour.

"Quite a contrast to the open fields and beaches of Cornwall," said Mum as we went back inside to take the lift up to the first floor.

A boy in a red uniform took our cases, accompanied us in the lift and along a corridor, and then unlocked our rooms and gave us our key cards.

"Wow," I said after he'd gone. "Cool."

My room was gorgeous. It had a massive bed, big enough for three people, with a maroon silk bedspread and six plump pillows, a telly, minibar, writing desk, comfy maroon chair, matching curtains, pale honey-colored walls, and an immaculate deep cream carpet that made you feel sinful to step on it.

Dad grinned. "*And* you get your own bathroom. Look, Becca," he said, gesturing toward the bathroom door.

"We'll leave you to it," said Mum. "Just knock if you need anything, as we're only next door. Meet you in an hour and we'll start exploring."

I nodded. It was good to see Mum smiling again.

As soon as I was alone, I went into the bathroom. It was huge. Almost as big as my bedroom at home, with marbled floors and surfaces, a double sink with wall-to-wall mirror, and an enormous bath with gold taps. I began to run water into it, to which I added a liberal splosh of the bath gel that had been laid out on the edge, along with shampoo and conditioner. It smelled divine—of orange and spices. And then I sang my head off as I had my bath. First my vocal exercises, and then all the happy songs I knew to reflect my mood.

Twenty minutes later, I was wrapped in the fluffy white bathrobe, lying against the pillows on the vast bed whilst flicking channels on my TV. I had a bar of chocolate and packet of nuts in hand from the mini-bar. It was bliss. I felt like a princess.

When I got my phone out to text Cat and Lia, it bleeped to tell me I had a message waiting.

MISS U, LAL XXXX, it said.

I quickly texted back. I MISS U 2. X

But oops—I didn't miss him. In fact, I'd forgotten all about him. There was far too much groovy stuff happening where I was to be moping over someone a million miles away.

• • •

We spent the first evening having a walk around the Old Town Square. It was a shock at first after the haven of our hotel, as it was packed with about a billion people and at least half of them were Italians traveling in large groups of twenty or thirty. But the square was very picturesque, lined with old buildings and churches that looked about a squillion years old. Dad explained that the architecture was a mix of styles—baroque, art nouveau, Gothic, Renaissance . . . I didn't care. I wanted to get back to the hotel, as I found the number of people milling about over-whelming. Even more so than when I'd been up to London and gone shopping along Oxford Street.

Saturday got off to a fab start. We were treated like royalty at breakfast. Everything was on offer: croissants, fruits, cereals, yogurt, bacon, eggs, mushrooms—whatever you wanted. I had muffins and apricot jam, hot chocolate, coffee brought to me in my own silver pot, and another pot of hot milk. And the waiter was so cute, with dark hair to his shoulders and smoldering dark brown eyes. He looked about nineteen and was every bit my idea of a Czech prince. If I hadn't been with Mum and Dad

I would have been more flirty but I wasn't going to do it in front of them in case they noticed and started teasing me. I almost texted Cat to tell her about him, but thought I'd better not; she might tell her new friend Lucy and she might tell Lal.

It was lovely and sunny and we spent the rest of the day exploring. I was glad I had taken my trainers, because boy did we walk. And walk. And walk. Church after church. Church of St. Nicholas. St. Peter. St. Vitus. Seemed like everyone had a church named after them. Old building after old building. Museum after museum. It was a nice city. Old and pretty with a fairy-tale look in some parts, but after a few hours, I began to get bored. I mean, how many churches did we need to go into? They all looked similar after the first five.

The Charles Bridge was more interesting.

Dad looked at his book as we approached one of the huge towers looming over one end of it. "The bridge is built in Gothic style and the statues lining the sides are baroque."

I tried to look interested, but history isn't really my thing. I was more intrigued by the souvenir stalls lining the sides, the musicians playing, and artists drawing portraits of tourists. At least they were alive, unlike the spooky black statues towering over us as we walked across to the other side.

"The most famous of the statues," Dad continued as we walked on, "is St. John of Nepomuk, a Czech martyr who was thrown to his death off the bridge."

"That wasn't very nice," I said as I stood on my tiptoes and looked over the wall into the river flowing beneath us.

"No, it wasn't," said Dad. "All the same, apparently tourists touch his statue for good luck."

When we found St. John, Mum and Dad went to touch him, but I didn't. I reckoned that if he was thrown off the bridge to his death, he hadn't had a lot of luck himself, never mind a surplus to pass on to a bunch of people he didn't know.

Once over the bridge, I found what soon became my favorite part of Prague. On the cobbled streets that led up to the castle, there were loads of little shops selling knickknacks, paintings, and all sorts of interesting stuff. I bought Cat and Lia presents there: tiny blue glass perfume bottles covered in silver mesh, one with the initial *C* on it and one with the initial *L*. Dad bought me one too with the initial *R* for Rebecca on it, as he said that I shouldn't be left out and it could be my souvenir of Prague.

We bought slices of pizza from a stall and ate them as we walked along in the sunshine. At last, it felt like we were a happy family again.

After the shops, it was up to the castle and more big halls, *more* churches, statues, and paintings of a load of dead people with miserable faces. It was okay for a while, but what I really wanted to do was to get back to our fab hotel where I could take another luxury bath, listen to some music on my iPod, and maybe order something from room service, which would hopefully be brought to me by the Czech prince waiter. In my mind, he would fall onto one knee and tell me that he had been waiting for me all his life and had found me at last. He might even burst into song. We might even do a duet. We would then have a great snogging session on the bed and then eat the rest of the chocolate from the mini-bar . . . or something like that.

But no such luck. Mum and Dad wanted to walk

round some more, so I trailed after them whilst texting Cat, Lia, and Lal, being careful not to say anything about the Czech prince. . . .

At about four, at last we appeared to be heading back to the hotel.

"So where shall we eat this evening?" asked Mum as we waited for a tram to pass so that we could cross the road.

"Oh, let's eat at the hotel again," I said. Last night's meal there had been delicious. Pumpkin risotto with cheese and pistachio crème brulée that was out of this world scrumbocious.

Mum shook her head. "We only have the bed-and-breakfast package on the deal that your dad got," she said, "so we had to pay for dinner last night on top, and, seeing as it's probably the best hotel in Prague, it wasn't cheap."

"Actually, I booked somewhere special for tonight," said Dad. "It was going to be a surprise. I read about it in one of my travel guides. It's supposed to be wonderful; a genuine Bohemian experience."

I noticed Mum's back stiffen as he got his book out of his rucksack and showed us the review and picture.

I thought it looked really glam, but Mum shook her head. "No. We can't eat there. It's way too expensive."

"Once in a lifetime," said Dad. "Come on. When will we be here again?"

I could see that Mum was struggling to share his enthusiasm but was finding it difficult. Oh, please don't start rowing, I thought. Not after such a lovely day.

"There were so many places in the square that looked just fine," said Mum. "We could eat there and I'm sure the food will be just as good and much cheaper."

Dad looked disappointed. "But the ambience won't be," he said.

I remember only a year ago hearing my parents joke about the fact that, in their relationship, Dad was the accelerator and Mum was the brake. It was still true, but somehow they didn't find it funny anymore.

I could see the hotel not far away and walked ahead. "See you back there while you sort out the dining arrangements," I said and speeded up my pace. I didn't want to listen. I knew the triggers to their rows and the cost of things was always one of them.

I went straight up to my room and thought about running through my vocal exercises or some songs, but I didn't feel like singing. Not one bit. Not even a sad song. I called Lal's mobile to cheer myself up instead.

Switched off.

Huh, I thought. Clearly not missing me one bit, because if he was he'd have his phone switched on every second.

Next I tried Cat.

"Oh hi, Becca," said her dad. "You're in Prague, I believe?"

"Yeah. Is Cat there?"

"She's out with that new friend of hers who's down from London. TJ," said Mr. Kennedy. "I think a crowd of them have gone down to the beach."

I felt a stab of jealousy. Cat was *my* best friend and she was out with this TJ. When I tried her mobile, it was switched off. I hoped she wasn't going to get taken over by this new girl.

I called Lia. Luckily she was at home but all she did was gush about TJ and her mates and how they were all going up to Barton Hall for lunch tomorrow.

"And Lal and his sister too?"

"Yeah, both of them I think," said Lia. "They're all so cool. Like really good fun. TJ's other mates, Nesta and Izzie, arrived last night. Nesta is so gorgeous and so is Izzie, but in a different way. You're going to really like them."

Oh, am I? I asked myself after I'd hung up. I'm not so sure. They all sound full of themselves to me. Just because they're from a big city, everyone is falling-over-themselves impressed. Well, they're going to have to do a bit more than just turn up to get in with me!

Dad won over where we were going to eat and, after baths and getting dolled and perfumed up, we went to a restaurant further along the river from our hotel. Mum looked lovely, dressed in a long, black linen dress and red silk wrap, and she had her hair loose for a change. I wore my turquoise halter neck, black trousers, and strappy high heels.

"I'm with the best-looking girls in the city,"

said Dad as he ushered us into the restaurant.

Inside was totally gorgeous, like walking into another era, maybe the eighteenth century—well, old-fashioned-looking anyway. It had floor-to-ceiling windows looking out onto the river, lush, green velvet curtains, and chandeliers that looked like they must have cost a fortune even though they weren't switched on. The room was candlelit. There were white linen cloths on the tables, which were set with crystal and silver. I felt like I was on the set of a costume drama and should be wearing a long dress and choker and dancing the waltz.

"Soooo posh," I whispered to Dad. "Good choice." I was born to be very rich, I thought as a waitress showed us our table. I feel so comfortable in places like this.

"It's what we deserve, Duchess," Dad whispered back.

The food was scrummy, but there could have been a bit more of it and I still felt hungry afterwards. Tiny bits of yummy stuff were brought on enormous white plates. Little bites of interesting tastes, arranged like works of art. It seemed a shame to ruin the design by eating them. Then more pistachio crème brulée—it must be a Prague speciality—and little chocolates with coffee served in dinky little cups afterward.

Externally everything was tip-top beautiful and elegant but the atmosphere between Mum and Dad was awful—so cold. It wasn't like they were arguing or being nasty. They were being polite like: "Please pass the butter," "Thanks," "Would you like some more water?" It was horrible. I prattled on to fill the silences, talking about where we'd been and about people we'd seen. And they listened and responded to me but not to each other. They didn't even make eye contact. They'd clearly had an almighty great row when I was on the phone in my room and getting ready for dinner.

Later that night when I snuggled down in my gorgeous princess's bed, I felt very small and alone and had a bad feeling in the pit of my stomach that something in my life was about to change and I wasn't going to like it.

6   Homeward Bound

ON SUNDAY, IT WAS OBVIOUS that Mum and Dad hadn't kissed and made up. At breakfast, the silent atmosphere was worse than ever, and I had run out of things to say.

"Your mum and I thought you might like some girlie shopping time together this morning," said Dad.

"And this afternoon, I thought you might like to do a river trip with your dad," said Mum.

I nodded, kept my head down, and concentrated on my croissant. Message understood. Things were so bad between them that they didn't want to spend anymore time than necessary together, even though we were supposed to be on a family break. They'll sort things out when we get back to England and familiar territory, I tried to convince myself. It had been a mistake to think that three days in a different place would solve matters between them.

However, even though I told myself that everything would work itself out when they got back home and into their usual routines, I couldn't help but feel depressed. This was meant to be Dad's special treat to celebrate his book deal and he looked as fed up as I was. It didn't even cheer me up when the Czech prince waiter brought me a second croissant and smiled at me in a flirty way after Mum and Dad had left the table.

Mum did her best to be bright and cheerful when we hit the shops, enthusing over this top, those trousers, a pair of sandals, and so on, trying to help me choose an outfit for the festival. And for once she didn't quibble about the price of anything. She bought me a fab pair of white cowboy boots and didn't bat an eyelid when the sales assistant told her the cost.

I tried my best to get in the shopping mood. We used to have great days together when I was younger browsing and trying things on, but it felt all wrong this time and I couldn't help but feel that I was being bought off.

In the afternoon, Dad hid behind his nerdy tourist

persona and gave me a running commentary on where we were, what had happened, and when. He had really swotted up on his history and it was funny when other tourists started listening to him more than the boat tour guide. It was nice being out on the water and seeing Prague from a boat, but I couldn't help but think that surely Mum would have enjoyed this trip too. Something big was going on. The bad feeling in the pit of my stomach was still there and it didn't get any better when Mum feigned a headache that night so Dad and I had to eat alone in a restaurant in the square. Exactly the kind of place that she had wanted to go to the night before.

We talked about everything but what was happening. School, me going into Year Ten next year, local gossip, the state of the world, what I wanted to do when I grew up, Dad's book . . . but it was as if there was a giant elephant towering over us and we were both doing our utmost to ignore it. Part of me desperately wanted to ask what was going on, but another part feared what the answer might be. That part won.

The following morning when we flew back to

Bristol, it wasn't soon enough for me. Mum and Dad were still doing the polite-stranger act and it made me want to scream. I think I'd have preferred that they argued. At least it would have meant that they were communicating.

We arrived home about three in the afternoon and I'd already texted ahead to Lal, Cat, and Lia.

Lal was waiting outside for me at the house as we drew up.

"Ah. It's loverboy," said Dad, attempting a smile.

As soon as I'd dumped my stuff in our hall, I was out the door again and off with Lal. Neither Mum nor Dad objected, even though usually when we were back from a trip, they would insist that we sort out washing, settle back in, and get readjusted.

Lal and I headed down toward the Italian gardens at Cremyl and it was such a relief to be away from the awkward atmosphere. It had been suffocating. Lal was so pleased to see me and, as soon as he could, he pulled me behind a bush for a reunion snog.

"I have been doing my research while you've been away," he said with a grin. "All the places where we can hang out without being seen. I've sussed out about ten places all over the peninsula."

He launched in to kiss me and I responded for a while, but ultimately, I wasn't in the mood. I pushed him away after about twenty minutes.

"What's the matter?" he asked.

I shrugged. "Nothing. Just . . . let's walk for a bit. . . ."

He grabbed my hand and we walked through the maze of hedges and out to an area that overlooked the sea and the naval base over at Plymouth.

Lal filled me in on what he'd been doing while I was away and I heard all about TJ and Lucy and Izzie and Nesta and I swear he blushed when he mentioned Nesta.

"You fancy Nesta, don't you?" I blurted.

"Do not," he said and then paused for thought. "Actually I do. Who wouldn't? Wait until you see her. I'd be mad not to. She's drop-dead gorgeous. . . ."

I was about to clout him when he added, "Like you."

We lay on the grass and stared at the sky and snogged a bit more, but I couldn't get over the nagging feeling that something was terribly wrong. My mind was in an overdrive of dark thoughts. What was going to happen? Would there ever be other holiday breaks? Would I ever want to go on them? What was happening with Mum and Dad? And that led to all sorts of other questions. What was love? Did it ever last? What do you have to do to make it last? I glanced over at Lal. He looked like he was thinking deeply about life and stuff too.

I turned onto my side and propped myself up on my elbow. "What are you thinking about?" I asked as I traced his profile with my index finger.

"Oh you know," he said. "Whether to get an ice cream on the way back, vanilla or chocolate. Why? What were you thinking about?"

"Life. The love lottery. Is it luck or chance that you meet the right person? What life's all about? Do you ever think about stuff like that?"

Lal let out a guffaw. He soon stopped when he saw that I wasn't laughing. "Oh! You were serious?" He coughed and made his face go straight. And then he started laughing again. He pushed me over, climbed on top of me, pinned my arms down with his knees, and started tickling me. I wriggled beneath him and fought back for a while and when I stopped, he lay flat on top of me and kissed me.

As we lay there snogging, I realized that something had changed in me over the last few days. Now I needed someone to talk to who could listen, understand, and be sympathetic. It clearly wasn't going to be Lal Lovering. All he wanted to do was get physical. Shame there's not an older more mature version of you, I thought as we eventually got up and headed back.

As we got near to our house, I couldn't face going in. I was about to turn to Lal and ask if I could go back to Mac's with him when I saw the front door open and Dad came out carrying a case. For a moment, I felt confused. We'd only just got back and he'd taken the cases *out* of the car so why was he putting a case back in the boot?

I darted behind a bush and pulled Lal with me so that we couldn't be seen. He took this as a signal for a secret snog session, but I swiftly elbowed him in the abdomen and pushed him out of the way so that I could see.

Lal clutched my arm and bent over in pain. "Wha—?"

"*Shhhhh!*" I urged as I watched Dad get into the car. He put his hands on the steering wheel and stayed there for a few minutes staring into space.

Then he started the engine up, backed out of the driveway, and drove off.

7 Heartbreak

"WHERE'S HE GONE?" I demanded when I got inside.

"Oh . . . Becca. You're back," Mum replied. She was in the kitchen putting laundry into the washing machine. "Er . . . he's just gone to stay with a friend for a . . ."

"What friend? Why? When will he be back?"

"I don't know. But he hasn't—"

"What did you say to him that made him leave?"

Mum sighed. "Nothing."

"But you must have. I saw him take a case. He's never done that before. What's going to happen? Are you splitting up?"

Mum glanced at the window and I followed her gaze and noticed that Lal was hovering in the garden.

"Oh, for God's sake," I blurted and got up and went

out to find him. I pointed at the gate. "Lal. Go. Later."

Lal looked taken aback and for a second an expression of hurt flashed across his face. He nodded and gave me the thumbs-up. "Right . . . okay. Later," he mumbled. He gave me a forced grin, then he turned on his heel and headed off.

Holy crapoly, I thought as I watched him droop away with his jeans almost falling off his hips and those stooped shoulders of his, now I've upset him. I considered running after him and explaining but realized that I didn't know myself what was going on. I'd sort it with him later. I went back into Mum.

She had made herself a cup of tea and was sitting gazing out the window. She had the same look on her face that Dad had when I saw him sitting in the car before he drove off. Sad. Weary. Shocked.

"So where are we going to live? Are we going to have to sell up? I guess we will. Where will Dad live? Why has he gone and not you?"

Mum's eyes shone with tears when I said that, but I couldn't help myself. My world was crumbling and I was starting to feel major panic. "Nothing's been decided yet for definite," said Mum. "Your dad went because . . . oh Becca, you must know that things haven't been right for a long time now."

"I know that you nag Dad a lot when all he's been trying to do is make things right."

Mum's mouth tightened. "I can't talk about this now, Becca. Go to your room."

"Go to my room! I haven't even done anything and you're *grounding* me?"

"I'm not grounding you. I . . . I . . . before he went, your dad and I agreed we would talk to you about this together."

"Which is why he drove away, is it? Doesn't look like talking about it together to me. Why has he gone and not you?"

"Because he can work from anywhere and I need to be near Plymouth."

With those words, I felt like I had been kicked in the stomach. Dad had left us. Not just Mum. He'd left me too.

I didn't want to talk anymore either and ran upstairs to my bedroom where I slammed and locked the door. I fell on the bed and stared at the ceiling. So now we all look the same, I thought.

Mum staring out the kitchen window. Dad staring out the car window. And me staring at the ceiling. There was nothing to look forward to in my life. Holidays are supposed to be a fun time, but so far, this summer had sucked. Even the thought of the festival at Maker fields didn't fill me with any enthusiasm and I'd been looking forward to that as a gold star spot in my diary for months. Singing was the last thing I felt like doing at the moment.

I really needed someone to talk to.

I tried Cat. Her dad told me she was out with TJ.

I tried Lia. She was out with Squidge.

I tried Mac. He was out with Lucy, Izzie, and Nesta.

My world is falling apart, I thought. Even my friends are moving on without me. All out with the London girls—so cool. So sophisticated. I hate them. I bet all their parents are still together.

I wanted to cry, but no tears would come.

I wanted to scream, but no sound would come.

I wanted . . . wanted to *stop* feeling like *this*. Stretched to the limit from the inside out. Upside down. And sideways. Feeling like I was about to burst. And empty. All at the same time.

I wanted to talk to Dad. If Mum wouldn't talk to me, maybe he would. I was about to go downstairs when I heard the sound of Mum's voice. She was talking to someone on the phone. I crept to the top of the stairs and stayed as quiet as I could so I could listen.

". . . taking it very badly," she was saying. "She's very close to Ian."

There was a pause as she listened to someone on the other end.

"No. Neither of us want it to get unpleasant or have to use lawyers as we all know that they would be the only ones who would benefit. No. We're going to try and sort it out between us."

Pause.

"No. I think it's too late for that."

Mum must have felt my presence, because she glanced up and saw me at the top of the stairs. "I've got to go," she said into the phone. "Becca's here. Yes. I will. Thanks. Bye."

She put the phone down and came to the bottom of the stairs.

"How could he just go like that?" I asked. "Without even saying good-bye?"

"Your dad? But he'll be back in the morning. I was trying to tell you. He's gone to stay with Mike Peterson over in Kingsand for the night. He'll be back in the morning. We . . . we just needed a bit of space to clear our heads."

I couldn't help but notice how tired Mum looked and for a moment, I felt sorry for her and for the things I'd said.

"Can I have his number?" I asked.

"He'll be here in the morning, love," she said. "In the meantime, unpack your things and we'll sort everything out tomorrow."

I went back to my room and lay back down on the bed. I'm going to run away, I thought. That will show them.

I imagined their reactions when they realized that I'd gone. I'd go to Brighton. I've always wanted to go there. Or up to London. Or even back to Bristol, where we used to live before Dad lost his job in advertising. If I went missing, they might realize what an almighty mistake this was and make more of an effort. But was it an almighty mistake? They hadn't got on for months. Maybe even longer. Still I didn't have to be a part of it. As I planned my escape route and what I'd need to take, I closed my eyes and in seconds, I was asleep.

The next morning when I woke up, sunlight was streaming through my curtains and I was about to snuggle back down when I remembered. My life wasn't the same anymore. My parents were breaking up. We'd probably have to move house. Dad might move away. I might have to leave my friends. I felt hollow inside. Nothing was certain anymore.

I didn't have to wait too long to find out what was going on, as when I left my bedroom to go to the bathroom, I could smell coffee and I knew that Dad was downstairs. Mum didn't drink coffee, only Dad did, and he was very particular about grinding the beans himself. I felt tears fill my eyes as I realized I wouldn't smell that lovely familiar smell anymore. Mum's camomile tea stinks of washing-up water.

I grabbed my dressing gown and raced down the

stairs and into the kitchen. Dad was on his own with his back to me as he busied himself with his coffee machine.

"I want to go with you," I said. "You *have* to let me."

Dad turned and his expression was both tender and sad. "Oh, Becca . . ."

I went over to him, wrapped my arms around his waist and buried my head in his T-shirt, which smelled of a mixture of herbs from his vegetable garden, coffee, and lemon. Dad smell. "You *can't* go, Dad. Please don't go. You're my dad and we're meant to live in the same house."

Dad hugged me back for a few moments and then gently extracted me. He pulled out a chair from the table and urged me to sit down. He went to the back door.

"Carole," he called. "Becca's up."

Mum appeared at the back door, looked anxiously at Dad and then at me. She nodded briefly and the two of them came and sat down. It felt so weird. This was the table that we'd sat at a million times, for hurried, manic breakfasts, lazy Sunday lunches, afternoon teas, late-night suppers. And now it felt awkward. It felt unreal, like I was floating—not really there. My parents looked so uncomfortable. My stomach tightened into a huge knot. I *don't* want this to be happening, I thought. I want to close my eyes and it to all go away. I can't deal with feeling like this.

Mum nodded at Dad to say something. He glanced over at me, then back at Mum. They were clearly finding the situation as difficult as I was.

"Becca," Dad started. "You know that we both love you very much, don't you?"

I felt a lump in my throat and tears threatening to well up. I tried to nod. I couldn't even meet his eyes. "I know what you're going to say," I blurted. "You and Mum are breaking up. Where are you going to go?"

Dad took a deep breath. "For the time being, I think I'll stay at my sister Marion's."

"In *Bristol?* But that's *miles* away! I'll never see you. Why are *you* going?" I knew this would happen, I thought. It's going to be exactly like what happened with Mac. He was miserable for ages and ages and even though his dad promised Mac his own room in his house in London, his dad's new girlfriend moved in and she had a daughter, who got the room instead.

Dad glanced at Mum again, then back at me. "Because I can work from anywhere." He attempted a smile. "Have computer, will travel. Your mum needs to be here so she can get over to her job in Plymouth."

"I don't need to be here. I'm on holiday until September. I could come with you."

"I'll be back every week to see you at some time," said Dad. "Bristol's not that far away. An hour if the traffic is good."

"I'll take that as a no, then?" I said harshly. "Why can't I come with you? Have you got a new girl-friend?"

"No. *No*. Absolutely not."

I glanced up and Dad was looking pleadingly at Mum.

Mum reached over to take one of my hands. I snatched it back as if it had been scalded.

"Then why is this happening? Why?"

This time it was Mum's turn to take a deep

breath. "Sometimes in relationships people . . . people change. As your dad said, Becca, we both love you very much and that will never change. You're our daughter. But . . ."

Dad took over. "We don't feel we can live together anymore, Bec. We've tried. Both of us. And we decided in Prague that . . . well, it would be best to take a break for a while. . . ."

"A break as in temporary, or permanent?" I asked.

Dad hesitated. "We . . . we don't know yet."

"When will you know?" I asked.

"Soon, love," said Mum. "And you'll be the first to know what's happening at all times."

"But where will I live? Where will I go to school?"

"Nothing is going to change for you, Becca. You can stay here. You can stay at the same school. We think that is best for you at the moment. The least disruption the better. You have great friends here and you're doing well at school and I'll be back every week to see you until I find somewhere more permanent."

"No you won't."

"Yes, I will. Of course I will."

"Every week?"

"I promise," said Dad.

I dared to look up and meet his eyes to check that he really meant it. I'd never seen him look so sad in all of my life and I felt that my heart was going to break. This can't be happening, I thought as tears filled my eyes. This is the worst day of my whole life.

8 Blair Twitch Project

THIS TIME I REALLY DID run away.

I waited until Dad had gone, then I packed my rucksack with the essentials. Lip gloss, travel hairdryer, toothbrush, iPod, change of underwear, change of T-shirt, mobile phone (on which there were four messages to call Lal), recharger, and twenty-five pounds from my secret savings box that I keep hidden behind my shoes at the back of my wardrobe.

I peered out of the window at the sky. Another glorious day, so I wouldn't need heavy clothes—shorts and a T-shirt would do.

When I was ready, I crept down the stairs. I was going to take some fruit and bread from the kitchen, but I could hear Mum moving around in there so I changed my mind.

Adios, amigo, I thought as I opened the front door as quietly as I could and tiptoed out. I was going to do what Dad had done. Leave. Stay away until my head was clear. Grown-ups weren't the only ones who could do that, and if he can do it without so much as a good-bye like he did when we got back from Prague, so can I. Yeah. Let's see how they like it, I thought as I legged it down the road toward the bus stop.

Once on the bus for Cawsand, I thought about calling one of my mates to tell them what I was going to do. I'd talked on the phone to Cat and Lia a few times to catch up since I got back from Prague, but I hadn't told them how awful it had been with Mum and Dad. Even though they were my bestest friends, I was hesitant to tell them everything now in case they tried to talk me out of running away. They might not understand. They might think I was being a drama queen and what did they know about what I was going through? Lia's parents were Mr. and Mrs. Happily Ever After and so were Squidge's. And Cat's dad was about to marry his fiancée, Jen. And he'd adored Cat's mum before she died. So Cat didn't know about the pain of unhappy parents either. I didn't want anyone who didn't understand telling me what to do. No, thank you. Mac was the only one who would understand, but I wasn't risking calling him in case Lal was around. The last thing I needed at the moment was another day of snog-wrestling with him. I so wasn't in the mood.

When I reached Cawsand, I bought a Cornish pasty, an apple, and a Ribena Light, then walked out through the woods toward Penlee Point.

I've definitely picked the right place, I thought as I looked around at the dense wall of trees lining the lane and the canopy of branches overhead. No one would ever find me in here.

After walking straight ahead for about fifteen minutes, I spotted a narrow track leading to an opening in the trees to the right of the lane. That's where I'll set up camp, I decided, and headed off into the undergrowth.

I cleared a space of twigs and leaves and sat down.

Right, I thought. I have run away.

This is me having run away. Good. Great. This will show them.

Them. As in my parents. Mum and Dad. Soon to be Mum. Dad. As in, separate. No longer joined with an "and." I just can't believe it, I thought as I replayed in my mind the scene from this morning in our kitchen when they told me they were breaking up. I just couldn't take it in. This was the sort of thing that happened on the soaps. In *Neighbours* and *EastEnders*. Not in my life, where everything was supposed to be safe and certain and secure. "We don't feel we can live with each other anymore," Dad had said, and my stomach had churned with fear. If they could fall out of love with each other, they could stop loving me as well. It was too depressing.

As I sat there, I wished I had brought a book or magazine to look at, as it was a bit boring just staring at the bushes, feeling gloomy and thinking depressing thoughts. I don't do moody-broody. Usually. Not my thing at all.

I ate my pasty and apple and lay back to look up at the sky.

Clouds. More clouds.

Still a bit boring.

Maybe I should have gone a bit farther away, like over to Plymouth, I thought. But then if I changed my mind about staying out for the night and wanted to go home, I might not have been able to get back, as the last ferry goes about half past nine. Even though I had run away, I wanted the option of going home. The idea was just to scare my parents and show them that they weren't the only ones who could cause problems.

I stood up and practiced my singing exercises and then I imagined that I was in front of the audience at the Maker Festival. I bowed and went to stand in front of an imaginary microphone. What would be an appropriate song for this being out here in the woods? Hhmm, I thought as I searched through my inner library of songs. The classic hit by Gloria Gaynor immediately came to mind so I sang "I Will Survive" at the top of my lungs. It usually made me feel better to sing something upbeat like that, but halfway through the song, I began to think, what if some poor unsuspecting soul was out walking their dog and heard me singing like a mad lunatic. It might scare the living daylights out of them. So I shut up and decided to do something that wouldn't attract the attention of anyone passing by.

I sat back down and listened to my iPod for a

while. I wished I had brought something to sit on. The ground was hard and little stones and bits of bark were sticking into the back of my legs. I tried to ignore them and relax. The sun was warm and after a while, I removed the iPod and drifted off to sleep.

Some time later I woke with a shiver. The wind had picked up and dark clouds had appeared in the sky. *Oh no*, I thought. *It's going to rain.* Just my luck. But that won't make me go back. Well, not yet anyway. A little rain never hurt anyone. I am strong. I shall survive . . . and all that.

I drank half of my Ribena Light, turned my iPod back on, and listened for a while on song shuffle. Above me, the clouds continued to gather. I glanced around. The fringe of dappled foliage that had earlier welcomed me had now become a wall of jagged shadows. Then it hit me. If anyone was around, I wouldn't be able to hear them over the music. I snatched off my headphones, trying to ignore the fear building in the pit of my stomach. Behind me, a couple of crows cawed and flapped off into the sky. I jumped to my feet. Get a grip, I told myself.

"Stupid birds," I said out loud.

I checked my watch. One o'clock. It felt like I'd been in there for hours. I took another slurp of my Ribena, then grabbed my headphones and threw them in my rucksack. I looked at what I'd brought with me. A hairdryer? How dumb can you get, Becca? I asked myself. Like I was going to find a n outlet out here in the woods. Ditto the mobile phone charger. And I knew the battery was low before I left home. Stupid. I'm not thinking straight, I told myself. It's Mum and Dad's fault. If I get murdered out here they'll have to live with that all their lives. And good job too. Tabloid headlines formed in my mind. *Teen runaway found dead in Penlee Woods. She ran . . . but not fast enough.* They'd probably use the rotten photo that was taken when I came third in the Pop Princess competition. It was in a number of local papers earlier this year. I'd die of embarrassment. Haha. Die of embarrassment. Cat and Lia would be devastated and realize that they'd been so busy with their new London mates that they hadn't noticed how unhappy I was. Ha. Me being dead would show them. And Mum and Dad would never forgive themselves, as they'd know that they were to blame for my premature and horrible end. They'd wear black for years and Dad would abandon the book he's writing and only write books about me called *My Duchess*, Volumes One, Two, Three, and Four. Lal would be heartbroken and write tortured poetry about the pale girl with red hair who haunted his days and nights.

As I began to picture my funeral and considered whether I'd like to be buried or cremated, another thought hit me. Maybe being out in the woods on my own *wasn't* such a good idea. Suddenly all the classes we'd had at school about being streetwise came flooding back. No one had mentioned being "woodwise."

The survival mantras ran through my mind: *Don't go into isolated places where no one could hear if you called for help. Stay on well-lit busy streets where you can be seen and heard.*

I looked around at my surroundings. Shadowy. Plenty of places for people to hide and jump out. Definitely an isolated place.

Oops.

Oh, get a life, I told myself. I'm okay. No one ever comes down here, apart from people walking their dogs and the odd miserable-looking jogger.

Exactly, said an ominous voice at the back of my head. No one ever comes down here. No one could hear you screeeeaaaammm.

Just then, the blackest cloud in the sky blotted out the last weak rays of the sun and the temperature dropped dramatically.

I shivered and gulped down my rising panic. No. I am not going back, I told myself. I have run away! I can't give up this easily. I tried to say it out loud to reassure myself, but my mouth was so dry only a croak came out.

I grabbed the Ribena and shook it. Empty!

The wind picked up and around me the branches began to creak and groan. I wished I'd brought my fleece. Another thing to add to the running-away list! I thought. I so wished I'd been more organized.

I'm scared, said the voice at the back of my head.

Oh, grow up, said a more confident voice. I've been in Penlee Woods a million times, with my mates, and with Mum and Dad.

Never on my own, though, said the quiet voice.

And then the wind dropped. Silence prevailed. Phew. I don't like the wind. I'll just call Cat and Lia and ask them to come and join me. Yes, that's what I'll do. They could bring supplies and we could have a laugh.

I stood up and, as I pulled out my mobile, I noticed that my fingers were trembling.

Behind me, in the shadows to my right, I heard a sharp noise. A footstep? Ten more cracks in quick succession. Yes, that's the sound of twigs snapping. Definitely footsteps. Someone's there. Instinctively, I crouched down, making myself as small as possible. I listened, suddenly aware that my heart was thumping deafeningly in my chest. I held my breath.

Silence. Silence is good. No more twigs snapping.

Then the voice in my head cut in with a new thought.

Ohmigod. I'm being watched.

I grabbed my rucksack and fled for the cover of a large bush. *Bedunk, bedunk, bedunk* pounded my heart. "Shut *up*," I whispered. "You're making too much noise."

A gust of wind rustled the trees behind me and my heart almost jumped into my mouth, and started to beat even faster. My breathing became short and sharp as I strained to hear the tiniest sound. I was surrounded by eerie noises. The soft, deep moan of the wind, the rustling of dry leaves, creaking branches, snapping twigs, and, in the distance, the boom of the sea breaking on the rocks.

I sooooo wished that I hadn't seen *The Blair Witch Project* on the night of Squidge's barbie. It's one thing watching something like that with your mates and a bowl of popcorn and another when you're alone in the woods and everything in the movie starts happening. I was a quivering mess, more Blair Twitch than Witch.

Another sharp crack from the shadows refocused my thoughts.

Now I was *really* frightened.

Running away wasn't my best idea, I thought. Maybe I should go home and rethink the plan.

A crack of brilliant lightning shattered the black sky and I picked up my rucksack and ran. As I reached the lane, the sky opened and large drops of rain sploshed down all around me. Soon I was soaked to the skin, hair plastered flat, black rivulets of mascara running down my face. I gulped for breath, but didn't stop until I reached the bus stop where, luckily, I didn't have too long to wait.

Mum was in the hall when I burst through the front door twenty minutes later. She looked surprised to see me.

"Becca! You've been out. Oh look, you're soaked. I . . . I thought you were up in your room." She gestured vaguely up the stairs and gave me a weak smile.

So much for the dramatic runaway scene, I thought as I dripped up the stairs. Ha! She hadn't even noticed I'd been gone.

<u>Revised Running Away Essentials:</u>

Waterproofs

Mobile (that has the batteries charged)

Lip gloss (*always* need that)

Groundsheet

Magazines

Food and drink supplies, especially chocolate
(lots of it)
Cricket bat for bashing suspicious people
over the head
Waterproof mascara
Fleece

Revised Running Away Philosophy

Don't bother

The Fab Four

SNOG. SNOG. SNOG. SNOG.

Cuddle. Cuddle. Cuddle. Cuddle.

Stroke hair. Stroke hair. Stroke hair. Stroke hair.

Zilch. Nada. Nothing.

It wasn't working.

I shoved Lal away.

"Wha . . . ?" he blustered.

I sat up. We had been lying on a blanket in the grass out in a field near Cremyl.

"I'm sorry, Lal, but I feel like I'm using you," I said.

"I don't mind. Really," he said with a wicked grin and stretched his arms out above his head. "Use me. Do what you like with me. I am at your service."

"I'm serious, Lal. It's doesn't feel right. I'm not myself. My mum and dad are breaking up and I'm freaked out of my mind, and sorry, but snogging you isn't taking my mind off it."

I stood up to walk away.

"Where are you going to go?" he called after me.

"Don't know," I replied.

I'm certainly not going home, I thought. After my pathetic runaway session I'd had some lunch, changed, and then called Lal. The weather had cleared and it was a lovely warm day again and I wanted to be outdoors (but not on my own in the woods anymore). Mum was going over to Plymouth to teach her classes for the afternoon and there was no sign of Dad, so there was no way I was going to stay in, moping at home. I'd thought Lal would be a good diversionary tactic from the black thoughts threatening to take me over, but no, it hadn't worked. I'd have to look for something else to take my mind off things.

Lal looked bewildered for a moment, then got up to follow me.

"Okay. I understand," he said when he caught up with me. "Well, sort of. Not really. One part of me will never get girls. But I wanted to say that if you feel like using me again, that it's fine by me. I'm used to being thumped about by girls when we have pillow fights. My sister and her mates do it all the time. I quite enjoy it."

"No. I can't. I don't know . . . I don't know what to do with myself. I . . . I think I need some time on my own."

I headed down the slope toward the lane at the bottom of the field.

"Come and meet the girls," said Lal running after me. "Izzie, Nesta, TJ, and Lucy. They're going to be on the beach this afternoon at Cawsand. I've told them all that you're my girlfriend and they're dying to meet you."

"No thanks," I said. "I'm not in the mood for meeting new people. I told you, I'm not myself. I want to be left alone."

Lia had texted me last night to say she was having a sleepover tonight up at Barton Hall and she was inviting the new crowd. A sort of Welcome to the Rame Peninsula pajama party, she'd said. I'd decided that I didn't want to go, as even though we hadn't met, I'd already had enough of the girls. I called them the Fab Four in my mind, because according to Cat and Lia, everything they did and said and wore was *fabulous*. I was getting so bored with hearing about them. And I also didn't want people coming into my life and asking questions like: Where do you live? And what do your parents do? What was I going to say? Don't know. Best to stay away, I thought, or else they'd soon realize how totally *un*fabulous I was.

Lal tried to catch my hand, but I snatched it away.

"I mean it, Lal. I want to be on my own."

Lal tried to hug me. "You need a hug," he said. "Come on and meet them. They're so cool. The coolest girls I know . . ."

If I hear that one more time I shall scream, I thought. Lia had been going on and *on* about how cool they were. And so had Cat. And so had Mac. Cool and fabulous. Cool and fab. Arrghhh.

"I have enough friends without making new ones," I said.

"Rubbish. There's always room for more friends. You'll have so much in common with them. Especially Izzie. She's got the *most* amazing voice and Mac told me that you can sing a bit too. . . ."

A bit? *A bit!* Only came third in a *national* competition

you eejit, I wanted to yell at him but he was still blabbering on about Izzie and her *amaaaaazing* voice.

Fab and cool and amazing . . . there was no end to how perfect these girls were. Fab Four. They had to be aliens. Or robots. They couldn't possibly be human.

"You and Iz can talk about singing," Lal continued, totally oblivious to the death-dart looks I was throwing at him. "Izzie is in a band up in London and Lia's dad has been trying to talk her into doing a number at the festival up at Maker or Raker next week."

Whaaadddddt? That was the last straw. *I* was supposed to be doing the solo spot there. It was my thing. Mr. Axford had promised it to me. And now this Izzie girl was going to do it? No! And already it sounds like she's in with the Axfords—singing, sleepover, cozy chats with Zac. It was too much! These girls were definitely taking over. No way was I going to go and meet them. I knew we wouldn't get on.

Lal was sidling up to hug me, but he looked nervous about actually doing it. I was feeling so cross about what he'd said about me singing "a bit" that I shoved him back so hard that he almost fell into a gorse bush, but he steadied himself just in time.

"Look, just leave me alone, will you? I don't even know why you're here. I'm horrible. I'm horrible to you. I'm not a nice person."

Lal grinned and rubbed his arms where I'd shoved him. "No, you're not. But who wants nice? You're great. Forceful . . . possibly the most forceful girl I've ever met but I *like* strong girls."

"You are mad," I said.

"Come on, let's wrestle," he said and took up a sumo wrestler's position opposite me. He tried to move in on me again and I shoved him off again but not as hard as before.

"Look. I mean it. All you want to do is snog me. There is more to life, you know. Like, I am going through a major crisis and all you can think about is sticking your tongue down my throat."

Lal grinned. "Can't help it. You're soooooo gorgeous." He knelt on the ground. "I am your slave. Use me. Use me. O mistress. I am helpless before your great beauty and my brain turns to mush."

He had clearly never read any of the "how to get a girl" manuals that tell you not to act desperate. All the same, I couldn't help but laugh. He looked so pathetic, kneeling there with his hands in the prayer position.

"Oh, all right. I mean . . . not the using you bit, but I'll come and meet your friends."

Lal bounced back up. "Great!" he said. Then he grabbed my hand and pulled me down the lane toward Cremyl.

Luckily, there was a bus right away, so we hopped on and got off at Cawsand. Lal took my hand as we approached the beach, then started blabbering on again about how fab the girls were. I began to wish I hadn't agreed to go with him. I so wasn't in the mood for meeting the Faaaaaaaaab Four.

As we got nearer, I began to feel inadequate. Never mind me liking them—what if they didn't like me? They were bound to be wearing some übergorgeous beach clothes and I was in a pair of old baggy shorts and an old pink T-shirt. I decided to act really cool with them and then make my exit as soon as I could.

Lal soon spotted the girls on the right side of the beach. Lucy was sitting up and she waved us over.

I did a quick assessment as we wound our way through the family groups on deck chairs and towels dotted along the sand. Even from a short distance, the girls stood out in a crowd. They looked like a beach shot from a fashion magazine. There was Lucy who was small, blonde, and pretty with a sweet, elfin face. She was wearing a white baseball cap, white bikini, and a white sarong. Very simple but chic. Next to her was the most stunning girl I'd ever seen and I almost turned and walked away right there and then. She had skin the color of fudge ice cream and looked like she'd just stepped out of Italian *Vogue*. I felt more intimidated than ever. She had long black hair tied back, cheekbones that could cut glass, and big black sunglasses, and she was wearing a straw cowboy hat, a tiny lime-green bikini and matching espadrilles. She had the most amazing body. Long, long legs and a perfect shape. I could see all the men sitting nearby sneaking glances at her. Even their wives were ogling. This was clearly Nesta. Next to her were the two other girls. They must be TJ and Izzie, I thought.

Lal picked up on my thoughts. "TJ's the one in the black bikini and Izzie's the one with the boobs in the turquoise."

They were striking too. TJ had long, dark hair

pulled back in a plait and Izzie had chestnut-colored shoulder-length hair. Both were tall and sophisticated looking. I wished I hadn't agreed to come. They were going to take one look at me and think I was a country bumpkin.

"Hi," said Lucy with a big smile when we finally reached them.

"Nesta, Izzie, TJ," said Lal, "this is Becca, the girl I was telling you about. She's back from Prague. And Lucy you met already."

Nesta took her glasses off to look at me and her jaw dropped open. "Ohmigod. *Ohmigod!*" she said as she stared at me open-mouthed.

I turned round to see if she'd seen something happening behind me. "What? *What?*" There didn't seem to be anything out of the ordinary happening on the beach and she was still gawping. Had I got a bogey on my nose? A wasp in my hair? What? What was she looking at?

Nesta shook Izzie. "Iz. Wake up. Open your eyes. Look who it is!"

Izzie opened her eyes and looked at me from where she was lying. Then she sat bolt upright and stared at me in the same way as Nesta had.

"Ohmigod! It's Becca Howard!" she said. "Lal! You didn't say you were seeing Becca *Howard*!"

I felt uncertain as to what to do. If this was some kind of joke that they'd decided to play, then I didn't think it was funny.

"Hi, Becca," said TJ. "Excuse my friends. I think that maybe they haven't taken their medication today."

Nesta half laughed, half snorted at her. "You don't know who this is, do you, TJ?"

TJ shook her head in an amused way, then nodded. "Er . . . Becca Howard. You just said. Lal's girlfriend?"

"'Scuse our friend," said Nesta. "She can be a bit of a dinosaur sometimes. Doesn't watch telly like us."

Lucy was looking as puzzled as I was. She turned to Nesta and said, "When your jaw has closed, do you think you could possibly fill the rest of us in?"

"Duh, Lucy. Becca Howard as in . . ." said Nesta. She leapt up and gave me a big hug. "*Pop Princess*! We voted for you in every round, didn't we, Iz?"

Izzie got up to join her. "Yeah. We thought you were *totally* the best and should have won."

Lal was grinning like an idiot and pu...
round me as if to say that he was proud to be with ...

"Ohmigod," said Lucy. "Of *course*. I should have
recognized you. You were soooo brilliant."

"You should never have come third," said Nesta.
"You were way better than the girl who won. I think
it was fixed."

"Yeah," said Izzie. "You have the *most* amazing
voice."

I couldn't help warming to them. "Oh. Thanks."
I'd expected them to be all looking down their noses
and arrogant, like we're it and you're not. But they
were exactly the opposite.

"God, you *have* to tell us all about it," said Izzie
and she took my hand to pull me to sit down next to
her. I noticed she had the most beautiful green eyes.
"I'm dying to ask you a million questions."

After that, there was no stopping us. We sent Lal
off to get us choc ices and we couldn't stop talking.
And they *were* cool. And fab. And amazing. But
what was most astonishing of all was that they
thought I was too.

Sleepover

"ARE YOU AN ONLY CHILD or have you got brothers and sisters?" asked Izzie.

"Do you live near here?" asked Nesta.

"What do your mum and dad do?" asked TJ.

All the questions I'd been dreading were coming at me and, funnily enough, I didn't mind anymore as they were so eager to know all about me. I felt like a celebrity.

It was later on the day that we'd met at Cawsand and we were sprawled out in Lia's bedroom, ready for the sleepover. Nesta, Izzie, and I were lying on Lia's princess bed with its floaty turquoise canopy above us. Lia and Lucy were sitting in her window seat and TJ and Cat were on beanbags on the floor. Lal had begged to be invited, insisting that sometimes up in London he was allowed to be an honorary girl, but Lucy put her foot down and told him that no boys were allowed and to clear off. He looked so sorry for himself when we waved good-bye down on the beach but his hangdog expression didn't persuade them to give in for a second. I was beginning to see why he didn't mind me bossing and shoving him about. He had it all a hundred times more from this lot.

As we settled in at Barton Hall and got changed into our jim-jams (Lia lent me a pair of pale blue ones with silver stars on them), I learned loads about the Fab Four. Nesta had a brother called Tony, who Lucy was in love with. Nesta had a boyfriend called William, who she was in love with. TJ had a boyfriend called Luke, who she was in love with. Izzie was the only single one.

I shook my head in answer to Izzie's question about brothers and sisters. "Nope, just me."

"Lucky you," said Lucy.

"What about you, Izzie?" I asked. "Are you an only child?"

"Nah, not really. It's complicated. I have two step-sisters and one stepbrother but none of them live with us. My mum and dad got divorced when I was nine. My dad remarried and they have a baby, Tom—so he's my half-brother and he's adorable. My mum married Angus and he had two daughters from his previous marriage, Claudia and Amelia. I used to hate him *and* them. I called him The Lodger and them the Ugly Stepsisters. I, of course, was Cinderella—misunderstood and never got to go the ball. But I like them all now. I was angry at Mum for ages for breaking up with Dad and blamed her for everything. I reckon that even if she'd married Mr. Perfect Hollywood Hunk, I'd still have hated him in the beginning."

"I think I'd be like that too," I said. "But what about you? Is there a boy that you're interested in?"

Lucy grinned cheekily at her friend.

"She likes the look of Mac. Don't you, Iz?" said Nesta.

Izzie slapped her friend's arm lightly. "Early days . . ."

At that moment, Mrs. Axford popped her head round the bedroom door. "Just checking, girls. Your parents all know you're here don't they?"

Cat, Izzie, TJ, Nesta, and Lucy nodded. I sort of

grunted. Actually, I hadn't told Mum. She wouldn't be back from Plymouth until after nine, so she wouldn't know that I wasn't tucked up in my room. And anyway, I didn't care what she thought. She hadn't even noticed that I'd been gone this morning, and last night when I'd wanted to talk, she'd told me to go to my room. Why should I tell her what I was doing?

"What about you, Becca?" asked Nesta after Mrs. Axford had shut the door. "What's your situation? Is it lurve with Lal?"

"Er . . ."

"Leave her," said Lucy, coming to my rescue. "You don't have to say Becca. Nesta is our token bigmouthed nosy git."

"Hey," said Nesta. "I was just asking. Taking an interest."

"I don't mind, Nesta," I said. Now that I'd got to know them, I wanted to talk. And it sounded like Izzie had been through something similar with her parents splitting up. "So. First question: my situation . . . ?"

And I was off. Once I started telling them what

was going on, I couldn't stop. I told them all about Prague. And about the rows. And about not wanting to go home. About worrying where my dad was going to end up and me not seeing him anymore. At one point, I felt close to tears and Cat and Lia immediately came to sit next to me and put their arms around me.

And then the pizzas arrived (only from downstairs—made by Meena, the Axfords' housekeeper). They were utterly scrummy—cheese, tomato and chorizo. After those, we had three tubs of chocolate-chip fudge ice cream between us. As we tucked in, I thought that I hadn't felt so happy in ages. The girls made me feel like it was normal to be going through such a major crisis. I felt accepted, and understood.

"It sounds like you're close to your dad," said TJ, "so it must be really hard for you. Recently when my dad was ill and I thought he might even die, I was freaked out of my mind. I didn't know what to do with myself. My mates really helped. They can see you through the hard times."

"Yeah," said Izzie, indicating Nesta, Lucy, and

TJ, "this lot have seen me through loads of bad times. And good."

"Me too," said Nesta as she draped herself Cleopatra-style over the bed and held her arm over her forehead à la tragic heroine. "Although most of my bad times have been over boys."

"I wish you'd told us what was happening," said Cat, looking at me. "I feel bad that you tried to handle it all by yourself."

"Yeah," said Lia. "I hate to think that you've been unhappy."

"I understand why she didn't let on," said Lucy. "Sometimes when you're in the middle of a freaky time, it can be hard to say what you're feeling without it coming out all wrong."

"Yeah," said TJ. "I do the classic thing of hiding it all away and have to be reminded that mates don't mind that you're not feeling up all the time."

"I *knew* something was wrong," said Cat. "But I didn't want to push you."

"Me too," said Lia. "I was really worried about you."

"Friends listen to what you say," said TJ. "Best friends listen to what you don't say. It sounds like your mates were listening to what you didn't say, Becca."

"I know and I'm sorry," I said. "I just thought you might not understand, because, well, Lia, your mum and dad are so happy and Cat, your dad is about to get married. I thought . . . I don't know what I thought . . . maybe that I was the only person going through this and . . . I didn't want to lay it all on you and be a killjoy . . . just as the summer hols were starting and everyone was in such a top mood."

Lia got up and joined us on the bed. "We'd have understood, Becca. You must always, *always* feel like you can come to us—no matter what."

Cat came and sat with her. "Yeah, and like TJ said, not just when you're up and fun. We love you for better or worse. . . ."

"For richer or poorer," said Cat, then put on a silly posh voice, "till death do us part. *Aaa*men."

I nodded. I felt a bit stupid. I should have known that Cat and Lia would be there for me.

Nesta grabbed a pillow from the head of the bed. "There is clearly only one way to get that message into her thick skull," she said.

Lia nodded and also grabbed a pillow.

"Yay! Pillow fight!" said Lucy, and leapt up to grab a cushion. "And I am pillow-fighting champion."

For the next ten minutes we had a great pillow-bashing session and when we collapsed on the floor afterward, I felt like I'd known these London girls for ever. They were so easy to be with.

It was a great sleepover. After the fight, Lia went downstairs for chocolate and Liquorice Allsorts and when she came back, she passed them round and then got out her beauty box so that we could do our nails.

We sat in a circle on the floor and in turn I did Izzie's nails, she did Lucy's, Lucy did Lia's, Lia did TJ's, TJ did Cat's, Cat did Nesta's, and Nesta did mine.

As we painted, pink, purple, and blue, we talked about all sorts of stuff and found we had loads in common: boys, beauty tips, hair, fashion, traveling, movies. We even liked the same books and authors.

"I so wish you guys lived nearer," I said.

"Ditto," chorused the girls.

After the makeover session, while we were waiting for our nails to dry, Cat suggested that we should have a homemade cabaret.

"Brill," said Lucy, "only I can't sing or dance."

She was game, though, and started off by doing a quick burst of mad Irish dancing while we all clapped and stomped our feet like mad.

Nesta was next and she did some fab flamenco while we all clapped again. She was amazing, graceful. A really good dancer.

Lia did some ballet and after a few minutes the rest of us got up and flapped away like fairy elephants behind her. It was so funny and I asked her to record it on her camera phone so I could show Dad. As she recorded us, an awful feeling of panic hit me in the pit of my stomach. Dad didn't live with Mum and me anymore. There would be no more getting home and bursting into his office to have a laugh over something that had happened. I pushed the feeling down. I didn't want the evening to be ruined.

Izzie taught us some Egyptian dance moves and Lia put on the song "Walk Like an Egyptian" and we all shuffled, wiggled, and wobbled round the room like idiots.

"TJ, you're next," said Nesta pulling her friend up from the beanbag where she'd collapsed after the belly dancing. "Come on."

"Oh, but I can't do anything . . ." she protested, then pointed at me. "Let Becca go next. She's not done anything."

"Yeah. Becca! Oh, sing, Becca," said Nesta. "Do the song you did for *Pop Princess*."

"But I need music," I said and acted the prima donna. "I can't possibly perform without my backing band and I have to have my own dressing room first, filled with *only* white flowers! So sorry, no. The conditions aren't right."

Nesta picked up a pillow and held it over me threateningly.

I held my arms over my head to protect myself, but she bashed me anyway. "Okay, okay, I'll sing. . . ." I said.

Lia leapt up. "Hold on. You want music? I have just the thing," she said. "Mum bought it last week for a laugh. Hold on a mo."

She dashed out and returned a few minutes later with a large box-type thing that she plugged it into the wall.

"Brill!" said Izzie. "It's a karaoke machine!"

Lia gave us a brochure that listed all the songs that were on the machine. We went down the list and sure enough, the song that I'd sung for the contest was there, "Nothing Compares 2 U." Lia found it on the machine so I stood up and did my song while they swayed along then joined in with the last chorus.

After that, there was no stopping us and we all got up to sing. Cat and I did songs from *Grease* while Lia did go-go dancing in the background. Nesta, TJ, Lucy, and Izzie soon joined her and the line of them dancing away looked hysterical.

We did all the usual songs: "I Will Survive," "Total Eclipse of the Heart," Kylie, Madonna, Mariah Carey, Britney, and no one cared about hitting the right notes or trying to impress anyone else—in fact TJ, Lia and Lucy were so off key, it made my eyes water. At one point, Lia's dad came in to see what the noise was and put his fingers in his ears, then bent over as if he was in agony.

Through it all, I could hear that Izzie really did have an amazing voice and when the others tired of howling away, Izzie and I warbled our way through "I Will Always Love You."

"Why didn't you go in for the Pop Princess competition?" I asked after we'd finished. "They had trials in London."

Izzie nodded. "I know. I found out about it too late and by the time I did, they were all ready into round two and not taking new people. But as we said, we watched it."

"You'd have easily got to the final," I said. "You have a great voice."

"So do you," said Izzie.

"You both do," said Lia.

"Izzie writes her own songs too, don't you, Izzie?" said Lucy.

Izzie nodded.

"Becca does too," said Lia,

"I'd love to see them sometime," said Izzie.

"Oh . . . but . . ."

"Hey, don't be modest," said Nesta. "If your song-writing is anything like as good as your voice, then it must be brilliant."

I noticed that Cat and Lia were staying very quiet, so I did too. The last thing I wanted to do was show any of my songs to anyone. In fact, since the beginning of the holidays, I'd hardly written anything except for two pathetic attempts—one about heroines and one about Henry. Songwriting wasn't like singing for me. Singing came easily. Songwriting was much harder.

"Hey," said Nesta. "I've just had the most brilliant idea. Why don't you and Izzie do a duet for the Maker Festival? What do you think?"

I glanced over at Izzie and she nodded. "God. Yeah, I'd *love* to. What do you think, Becca? Would you mind me singing with you? But if you're up for doing a solo spot, I don't want to steal your thunder or anything."

I thought about it for a moment. Did I care about having a solo spot? Not really. It was the singing that I enjoyed more than anything. It was the one time when I felt that I was completely alive and could express my feelings. I didn't need to have all the limelight and singing in public with Izzie might be fun.

"I think I'd love it if we did a duet," I said with a grin.

"Excellent," said Nesta. "Now, everyone up for the Greek Zorba dance."

We all got up, put our hands on each other's shoulders, and did Greek dancing round the room. Then Lucy started giggling, which set the rest of us off and we had to lie on the bed, where I laughed until my jaw ached.

It was then that Mrs. Axford put her head round the door and said, "Er, Becca. Your mum's on the phone. . . ."

Oops, I thought.

Past Times

"WHY DIDN'T YOU KEEP your mobile on?" "Why didn't you let me know where you were?" "How was I supposed to know that you were up at Lia's?" "Who else was there?" "Did you get supper?" "Do you think I'm psychic or what?"

Mum hit me with a barrage of questions when I walked through the door the next morning. She'd allowed me to stay on at Lia's for the sleepover, but boy was I in the doghouse when I got home. I'd tried to time it so that she would have left for work, but her shifts were different in the summer and she was only working afternoons this week.

She was waiting for me with tired eyes and an angry expression. Nag, nag, nag. No wonder Dad was leaving her, I thought as she started on me and wouldn't stop. She'd phoned round everywhere, woken up Cat's dad, woken up Mac's gran, who had gone to

Lal and found out from him that I was up at Lia's.

"I don't know what you're getting so het up about," I said. "I mean I've stayed at Lia's a million times and you've never bothered before."

"Only because you *told* me that you were there before."

"Where else am I going to go?" I said. "You should have known."

Wrong thing to say. Mum's mouth tightened and she looked like she was about to let rip . . . when suddenly her shoulders slumped and she looked like someone had let the air out of her.

She reached across the table and put her hand on mine. "I know you're not happy about what's happening at the moment, Becca. This is a difficult time for all of us and I wanted to be sure that you were okay."

I pulled my hand away from under hers and crossed my arms over my stomach. "I'm fine. I have my friends at least."

Mum sighed and got up. "I have to get going, Becca," she said. "I've got a dental appointment in the village. How about we do something when I'm back. Go for a walk or a coffee or something before I go over to Plymouth?"

I shrugged. "Got plans already. I may do something with Lal or the London girls. They're only here for a short time."

"Oh, you've made friends with them, have you?" asked Mum with a glimmer of a smile.

"A bit." I didn't want to get into details with her. I knew I was being uncommunicative, but I couldn't help it. Part of me still felt that she was to blame about Dad leaving and I wasn't in the mood for being all pally-wally friends with her, as if everything was hunky-dory when in fact she'd ruined our lives.

After Mum had gone, I went up to her and dad's bedroom to see if he'd taken anymore things. He had, which meant that he must have been back yesterday when I was out. He hadn't taken all his clothes, but there were definitely gaps in the hanging space in the wardrobe where his shirts and trousers had been. One of the drawers in the chest of drawers was empty.

I sat on their bed, smoothed down the bedspread

on Dad's side and wondered if Mum felt lonely in such a big bed on her own.

In the bathroom, Dad's toothbrush had gone. I felt a stab of sadness when I saw two toothbrushes in the glass instead of three—my pink one and Mum's red one. Dad's had been blue. His would be lonely on its own in a strange bathroom. I looked around to see what else had gone—his soap bag, shaving stuff. I opened the cabinet above the bath and found a bottle of his aftershave lotion tucked behind cotton buds and shampoo. Only a bit left in the bottom. I pulled the bottle out and sprayed. The scent of lime and sandalwood filled the air. The smell of Dad. I took the bottle into my bedroom and hid it under my mattress in case he moved far away and I needed reminding of him.

I wandered round the rest of the house, looking for evidence of Dad and wondering what it would be like when he'd really moved out. Already the house felt quieter.

His office was untouched, his computer in its usual place, books and files on the shelves. He must be coming back for all this, I thought, feeling glad that he hadn't completely left yet.

After mooching through his office, I went into our living room and opened the cupboards in there. Books, videos, DVDs, CDs, photo albums. How were they going to decide who got what? As I sat on the floor to have a closer look at what was in there, I thought that breaking up when you've lived together for a long time must be really difficult. It's not like dating someone and then dumping them. If you've lived together, there are so many shared things. And what if you have pets? You can't split a cat or a dog or a goldfish down the middle. On second thought, I guess you could . . . but it wouldn't be very nice.

I had an hour before I'd arranged to meet Lal in Cawsand, so I put on one of Mum's love ballad CDs, pulled the photo albums out onto the floor, and sat down to look through them. Mum was always so good at putting them into books and labeling them with the year and the place.

First I looked at the one with Mum and Dad BB— i.e. Before Becca. It was weird to think that this world and these people existed before I was born. There were loads of Mum as a teenager, my age—one of her in a garden, laughing into the camera; one of her bent over a book studying. She looked so different. Whatever happened to that person? I wondered as I turned the pages. She looked so full of joy and now she looked sad, serious, and care-ridden. Like life had worn her down.

Halfway through the album there were shots of Mum and Dad when they were at university, which is where they met. Dad looked so young—barely older than Mac and Squidge. Some shots showed him with a moustache. Ewww. I'm glad he got rid of that, I thought—it looked like he had a caterpillar under his nose. There were pics of Mum with long, straight hair, then a perm, then dressed in the power suits and big jewelry that were so popular in the eighties. There were a couple of pages of wedding pictures with Mum gazing lovingly into Dad's eyes. She looked so pretty with her hair tied up, laughing as wedding guests threw confetti over them. They looked happy. Then a holiday by the sea somewhere—I think it was Spain they went to for their honeymoon—Mum in a bikini, Dad in a hammock in a garden. Then back in the UK, Dad standing with a sports car outside the advertising agency where he worked in Bristol, Mum with wellies and a watering can the garden. Smiling. Happy days.

I lifted the next album on to my knee. Ah, along comes baby me, beaming parents holding me in their arms. In the garden, toddling into flower beds. School, holding Dad's hand and looking miserable because I didn't want to go in. Shots of me in the school production of *The Wizard of Oz*. I was Dorothy. That's when I first got a taste for performing and realized I could sing. "Somewhere Over the Rainbow" was my party piece at family gatherings until I grew older and thought it way uncool.

I began to feel desolate as I pored over the albums whilst listening to the music. One song after another about lost love, the pain of love, the loneliness of love. I sang along with the ones I knew as I looked through the pages. Some of the lyrics expressed the whole situation perfectly and I marveled at how songs could do that. I could never understand people who didn't have time for music.

For me, it was a release, a solace, a reassurance that I wasn't alone in what I was experiencing, whether it be happiness or sadness.

I pulled out the last of the photo albums. Birthdays, Christmases, family holidays—how could they have forgotten these times? A whole lifetime of happiness was here in pictures. I remembered it all. We were all happy. I'm not imagining it. I remembered Mum and Dad snuggling up on the sofa and me coming home from school once and catching them. They sprang apart then started giggling like school kids. That had been a long time ago. When did it all go so wrong? And how were they ever going to split up these albums into his and hers?

As I flicked through the pages, I tried to work out when the smiles disappeared. Was it when Dad lost his job in advertising and we moved down here to live? I wondered. I think it was. They've forgotten that they were happy. They've forgotten that they loved each other. I must remind them, I decided as I hauled the albums onto the kitchen table. If only Mum could change. Be happier again, it could work. I didn't want her to be without Dad and I didn't want Dad to be without her. They were meant to be together. Anyone who looked at the photos could see that.

Before I went out, I took the CD out of the player and left it with a note, saying, *Dear Mum (and Dad, if you come by today), look at these whilst listening to this CD. How can you have forgotten all of this? Why are you splitting up? You must be mad. Your loving daughter, Becca.*

I called Dad to make sure that he *would* come over today and got his voice mail. "I've left something for you on the kitchen table," I said into the phone.

And then I ran off to meet Lal. I didn't want to stay in our house any longer. It felt too quiet and empty, as if everyone had already moved on.

Double Vision 12

SNOG. SNOG . . . OH HERE we go again.

I pushed Lal off, extracted myself from his limpetlike grasp, sat up, and looked out to sea at Cawsand Bay. I had to face it—it just wasn't happening for me with him anymore. No fireworks. No tip-to-toes tingles. He'd got me at a vulnerable moment. If only I hadn't fallen for Squidge's dare to kiss the first boy we saw on the beach, I'd have never got into this mess.

"Er . . . when are you going back to London?" I asked, trying to sound casual. I was hoping that it was soon, because I hated finishing with people. I hate hurting their feelings and, despite having cooled off in the snog department, I did like Lal as a person. As a friend. Soon to be long-distance friend.

Lal gave me a suspicious look. "Not sure. Why? Are you tired of me?"

I hoped that I wasn't blushing, but I had a feeling that I was. I took a deep breath and reached out for Lal's hand.

"Listen, Lal, I really like you. . . ."

He snatched his hand back and put an index finger into each ear. "*Arghhh.* Oh God, here we go with the 'I really like you' conversation. I don't want to hear it, *don't want to hear.* Too soon. Too soon."

I pulled his hands away from his head. "Listen, idiot, I'm not dumping you."

I wasn't. I'd decided that I couldn't do it yet. With everyone at home moping about, being miserable, I didn't want another person in my life to be walking around with a face like a rainy day. He'd be gone soon, and besides, I didn't want to ruin his holiday. I may be fickle but I'm not mean.

"So what, then?" asked Lal. "What's going on? And *please* don't give me the 'I like you as a friend' line."

I burst out laughing.

"Why are you laughing?" asked Lal.

"Oh, nothing . . ." I couldn't tell him that I'd been thinking of using *exactly* that line.

"So what's the matter?"

"Nothing, I guess . . ."

Lal sighed. "I really, *really* don't get girls. You are such a strange species."

"Not strange, just . . . complex. That's what makes us interesting. So seriously, when are you going back?"

"In a week or so. Soon after the Maker Festival as Dad has to get back to his shop and Mum has clients to see. I might stay longer. Dunno yet. I could camp maybe. Everyone loves it down here. Can you believe Mum and Dad have been checking out properties too?"

I felt a rising panic. Oh noooooo. Don't let him come and live down here.

"But no way can they afford anything," Lal continued as I sighed inwardly with relief. "TJ's parents are much richer than mine, both being doctors. My mum and dad don't earn that much. I think we could probably afford an old, battered caravan up at Whitsand and that would be it."

"What a shame," I lied, thinking, Phew, phew, *pheee*-ew.

"So what did you want to say?" asked Lal.

"Just that I'm sorry if I've been behaving a bit strangely of late. I'm not my normal self."

"Girls never are," said Lal. "That's what makes them a different species. Like, with a boy, you know where you are. Same person most of the time— steady, consistent. But a girl, Jesus, she can go from saint to sinner, cool to bonkers and back in five minutes. That's why I think it's best not to talk too much. Only confuses things. Best to just use the language of love."

He closed his eyes, pursed his lips and moved in for another snog.

"And do you understand 'no' in the language of love?" I asked as I pushed him away.

Lal opened his eyes then shrugged. "I guess. Want an ice cream?"

I nodded. "I'll come with you."

When we got to the café at the top of the beach, Cat was standing in the ice cream queue with her little sister, Emily. Both of them waved when they saw us.

"Hey, Em," I said.

"Hey, Bec."

"This is Lal," I said.

"Hi, Emily," said Lal.

"Hi," she said. "I need to pee."

I laughed. "Well, there's a chat-up line if I ever I heard one."

Cat looked at the queue and then at Emily, then at Lal.

"Er . . . would you mind, Lal? I want to keep my place and need a word with Bec. The ladies' is just back there, down the alley."

Lal looked totally horrified. "What—me?"

Emily was gazing up at him adoringly. "You're a great man," she said. "I like you."

I gave him my best smile. "Brownie points, big boy."

Lal sighed and held his hand out to Emily. "Come on, kid."

He walked off with her, muttering something about bossy women and how other boys managed.

"So, how's it going?" asked Cat as soon as he was gone.

"Honest?"

"Honest," said Cat.

"I think our relationship has run its course, but I

haven't the heart to tell him. I can't bear another miserable face in my life."

"Have you tried?" asked Cat. "Because it might be like when you wanted to finish with Mac and were agonising over it and in the end he'd been thinking the same thing all along."

An image of Lal, eyes closed, lips pursed, came into my mind and I shook my head. "No. Really, Cat. He's still into me. My plan is to hang out with him until he goes back and then let him down gently. I mean, he'll be up in London. I'll be down here. It shouldn't be a problem, and then I can say I've met someone else or something."

"How's it going otherwise today?" Cat asked. "At home?"

I let out a long breath. "Weird. Quiet. When Dad was home, you always knew it. You could hear him, either talking on the phone or putting the kettle on or Radio 4 would be playing. I miss him."

"How's your mum?" asked Cat.

"Don't know. Don't care."

"Becca! That's awful. Why don't you care?"

"It's all her fault. She pushed him away. . . ."

"No. *No*," said Cat. "I'm sure it wasn't like that. It takes two to make it work and it takes two to end it."

"Since when are you the relationship expert?" I asked.

"I'm not, but . . . well, I know your mum and she's nice. So's your dad, but I can't see that she'd drive him away on purpose."

"You don't know. You haven't lived with her. She's always on at him, belittling him, always about money."

"I read that finances are one of the top things that break couples up. I'm going to make sure that I always have my own career and finances so that I'm not dependent on a man."

"Me too," I said. "Although I won't mind if a guy is megarich and wants to treat me to the best. I'll just make sure I have backup money too. Thing is, Mum has been the breadwinner for so long, and I think Dad has felt bad about it. But now he's got his book deal things should have got better as he'll be earning again, but things have just got worse. Really, Cat—it's her, not him."

Cat looked wistful for a moment. "Give her a break, Becca. It can't have been easy for her these last years. And . . . you're lucky to have a mum. She's kept it together for you all this time—like, imagine if your dad had lost his job and your mum *hadn't* been able to pay the bills. What would have happened?"

"Yeah, but . . . but she needn't rub everyone's face in it all the time."

"Just give her a break," Cat said again. "I reckon there are always two sides to a story. And, well . . . you only get one mum."

"Suppose," I said with a shrug. I guessed Cat was sticking up for my mum because hers had died. For a moment I tried to imagine how it would have been if that had happened to me. Would I have missed her? And how would Dad and I have survived? God. It must have been awful for Cat, I thought. I know Mum and I don't get on sometimes but I couldn't imagine life without her.

My thoughts were interrupted by a strange sight coming round the corner by the alley. I rubbed my eyes, as I thought I had double vision and was seeing things.

"Cat. *Cat.* Look. Over there at Lal. Ohmigod. He's duplicated himself!"

Cat laughed and glanced over to where Lal was approaching us, still hand in hand with Emily but on her other side, holding her other hand was a taller, older-looking version of Lal.

"Dingbat," said Cat. "That's his brother, Steve. He arrived last night."

"Steve?" I vaguely remembered Lal telling me something about an older brother, but somehow I'd imagined that he'd be a lot older, like in his twenties, whereas the boy who had just arrived in front of me looked about eighteen and was very, very cute, in a Harry Potter kind of way with shoulder-length dark hair and hazel brown eyes behind his glasses.

For a moment, I totally lost my cool and pointed at him. "You brother . . ." I muttered sounding as if I was in a Tarzan movie—Me Tarzan. You Jane. Me Becca. You Steve. Ug.

Lal grinned. "Yeah. He brother. Ugly specimen, isn't he? Steve, this is Becca. My *girlfriend*, Becca."

Steve looked unimpressed. "Hi," he said. "Lal's girlfriend, huh?"

"Yeah. No. Or at least yeah, but please don't hold that against me."

Steve almost smiled. "I'll try not to, but I have to question your taste."

"Really?" I said and gave him my best flirty look. "And would you question his?"

Steve shrugged and looked away as if he had lost interest in the conversation. I glanced over to check whether Lal had heard, but Emily was dragging him away by the hand toward the sea, so he was well out of earshot.

Cat had heard, though, and when Steve went to join Lal, she gave me a sharp dig in the ribs. "Chocolate or strawberry, Becca?" she asked in a clipped voice.

"Oh. Er . . . what flavor would you recommend, Steve?" I called.

"Whichever," he called back. "Vanilla."

"I'll have the same as Steve, then," I said to Cat.

Cat looked at me and then at Steve, and then rolled her eyes.

"For God's sake, Becca," she whispered. "He's Lal's brother."

"So?" I asked. "It's not as if he fell at my feet. In fact, I have never had a boy register such disinterest before. He's not like Lal at all, is he?"

"So what do you care?"

"Duh. He's major cute—or didn't you notice?"

"Don't you have *any* feelings?" asked Cat. "I don't know what's happening to you lately. You don't care about your mum. You don't care about flirting with Lal's older brother right under his nose. You're in danger of becoming heartless."

I felt horrible when she said that. "I do have feelings," I said. "Course I do. Lots of them. All over the place. Hundreds of them. But that's just it, Cat. I don't know what to do with them sometimes, so I push them down and put them in a box deep inside. . . ." Suddenly all those boxed-up feelings threatened to come roaring up to the surface. It really hurt to think that Cat thought I was heartless and I felt like I was going to cry. Cat saw immediately and put her arm around me.

"Hey, hey, come on. It's okay. It will be okay," she said.

"No, it won't. It will never be okay again and I

can't kid myself anymore by pretending that everything's all right, because it isn't."

Suddenly I wanted to get home. I didn't want to be out snogging Lal or flirting with his brother and I had no appetite for ice cream. I needed to talk to Mum or Dad and really face up to what was going to happen.

Get Him, Rover   13

DAD WAS IN THE KITCHEN when I got home. He had the photo albums and my note in front of him on the table.

"Where's Mum?" I asked.

"Not back yet," he replied, and then indicated the albums. "But I think we need to have a talk. Just the two of us. Don't you?"

I nodded slowly. I wanted to face up to the reality of what was happening, but inside, I felt like I was an innocent victim just about to be given a jail sentence.

Dad took a deep breath. "Listen, Becca, about your note . . ."

"Is it my fault?" I interrupted. "Did I do something to spoil things? Have I been too demanding? Been a bad daughter? Heartless? Only thinking of me? I know it was hard when I wanted to go up for the *Pop Princess* finals and you didn't have the money. . . ."

"No way is it your fault!" said Dad. "And you must get that thought out of your head right this instant. You'll understand when you get older. It's no one's fault, just sometimes feelings change."

"Tell me about it," I said. "I know all about feelings changing. I don't have to wait until I'm older!" I thought about all the boyfriends I'd had. All four of them. Phil Davies in Year Eight—a blip, but I had liked him when I was young and demented. Mac in Year Nine. Luckily, we're still mates. Henry, although we weren't anything serious. He was just a holiday romance. And Lal—another one soon to be an ex. "I know. It's hard letting people down, even when you're sure it's not working, but . . . with you and Mum it *did* work."

Dad nodded. "It did. For many years. But no one's let anyone down here—honestly. It's a mutual agreement. Both your mum and I want to split and we're going to stay friends. We really are—unlike some couples. We've had too many good years, as you've seen looking through the albums, to let it all go. In fact, when we're apart I think we'll be *better* friends."

"*Really?*" I wasn't convinced. Mac's mum and dad hadn't stayed friends. Far from it—they were barely on speaking terms. And Mrs. and Mr. Abbott that used to live next to the post office, they hadn't stayed friends either. I remember they'd had a great argument when they split up. She chucked him out with his cases and he was standing in the street, looking sad, with a whole crowd of nosy parkers looking on. He looked back at her and called out sadly, "Julie, any last words for me to remember you by?" And she said, "Yes. Get him, Rover."

"Sometimes in life, Bec," said Dad, "you have to accept that something isn't working and you have to let go of some aspects of what has become familiar and look for a way forward. It isn't as if we haven't tried to make it work." He let out a long sigh and ran his fingers through his hair. 'Do you think you can possibly understand?'

I thought for a moment. I thought about my songwriting. About how that wasn't working and about how I could keep plugging on with the lyrics when I knew that really they were worse than mediocre. Or I could move on. Accept that I had tried, but that I had limitations—that maybe songwriting wasn't for me. I was sure that there were other people on the planet who could write but not sing. Some lucky people could do both, but Dad was right. Sometimes in life, you have to accept what you can and can't do. Let go and move on.

"I do understand, Dad," I said. "Sometimes you have to let go and accept that something is not going the way you'd hoped. But what about me? I don't want you to go. I like having you here. It's not fair. I *like* living with you. . . ." I could feel the tears that I'd been holding back threatening to spill out. "I know what it can be like. I've seen it with Mac. His dad promised all sorts of things, but in reality, he hardly ever sees him and his dad has a new girlfriend. Mac doesn't even have his own room at his dad's place. . . ."

This ought to have been a cue for Dad to reassure me, but he just grinned.

"Dad! Why are you grinning like that? Are you so happy to have got away from us?"

"Not all relationships are the same. Not all marriages are the same. Not all divorces are either. What happened with Mac has nothing to do with us. For one thing, I haven't got a girlfriend. And for the record, I like living with you too."

He picked up a paper from the table and waved it at me.

"What are you doing for the rest of the day?" he asked.

"Not sure. Why?"

"Want to come and look at a property in Kingsand with me?"

"Property? Kingsand? What do you mean?"

"Well, if you're going to have a room with me as well as here with your mother, then I think you should give any place that I take your seal of approval, don't you?"

I felt confused. "Room with you? I thought you were going to Bristol to stay with your sister."

"Only for a couple of weeks! I was going to go up there, clear my head and have a think about things, but your mother and I know what we want in the long run. We talked about it in Prague and, to be perfectly honest with you, that wasn't the first time we'd discussed splitting up. Things haven't been right with us for a while. We did try to make it work, but now . . . well, we've both agreed that this is for the best. But I don't want to move away—that was never on the cards, and anyway, I love this area. The plan was to get a flat, house, whatever, as near as possible and for you to have a room there too."

"Near? Me? With you?"

"Yes. Of course. And you'll keep your room here with your mum. I thought it would take a while to find the right place, with it being the summer and most places already having been taken but something's come up. I saw old Dan Jason in the pub in Kingsand last night and we got talking. He has a few properties around the area and he'd just been let down by a tenant who was supposed to be moving in next week. Dan was in the pub cursing the man, but I saw an opportunity. . . ."

"You . . . you mean, you're going to get a place in Kingsand?"

Dad nodded. "Yes. This place could be perfect. I had a quick look this morning, but I want to know what you think. It has three bedrooms, so there's one for me, one for you, one for my office. And it's got lovely views looking out over the bay. It's the blue one up to the left of the village if you're looking out to sea."

"I think I know it! Not far from the fish-and-chip shop?"

Dad grinned. "Exactly. We might have landed on our feet, kid. Half the week, you can live with your mum and the other half the week you can live with me. You'll always have a room wherever I live—you know that, don't you? I'd always make sure of that." He pulled out a set of keys and waved them at me. "I've still got the keys, so we can go over and have a wander round and see what you think. You can see your room. But if you don't like it, we'll look for somewhere else."

An amazing feeling of happiness rushed up through me from the inside, like someone had switched on a heat source beneath me. As the surge of emotion rose from my stomach up to my throat, much to my surprise, I burst out crying.

"Becca! Oh. I thought you'd be pleased."

"I am . . ." I sobbed. "At least I think I am. I'm really, *really* happy. I feel like I've won the lottery or something. But . . . I'm . . . I'm confused . . . I thought you were going and I wasn't going to see you anymore and I had to be brave and act like I didn't care and be grown-up, because loads of people's parents have split up—it's not as if you've died or anything—but it felt like you'd gone, even though you're still here . . ." Another wave of tears engulfed me and I couldn't help but sob even louder. "Sorry. Sorry. I'm happy. Really, I am . . . and I love Kingsand. It's nearer to Squidge and Cat, too."

Dad started laughing then and so did I, then he gave me a big hug.

"I wouldn't leave my favorite girl behind now, would I?" he asked, which only set me off crying again. I felt like I was going mad. Happy, sad, crying, laughing. Totally mad.

When I'd calmed down, we got into his car and drove over to the village. Dad parked behind the pub and we bought enormous ice creams at the tea shop by the bay, then went to look at the house. I'd walked past it a thousand times on my way to Squidge's. It was painted pastel blue and had big bay windows with seats for sitting in to look out over the sea.

"I think I love it," I said as we wandered through the downstairs rooms and out onto the little terrace, which overlooked Kingsand Bay.

Upstairs were three bedrooms and a bathroom, all light and airy rooms with great views. I could easily see myself living here and Dad writing his books and looking out to sea. It'd be fab.

"But . . . what if Dan wants his house back?" I asked.

Dad shrugged. "Renting out property is how he makes his living, Bec, so I don't think he will for a while. He wants to let it on a long lease, saves all that coming and going of short holiday lets, never knowing if people are going to turn up or let you down at the last minute. He's so glad to have a long-term tenant that he's going to give it to me at a special rate. And if he does change his mind for any reason in the future, it'll be fine. I might look for somewhere to buy while I'm here. If the right place comes on the market, why not? Things change. Life changes. The only thing that doesn't change is you and me. I'm your dad and you're stuck with me for life."

I wrapped my arms round his waist and gave him a hug.

"I think we'll be very happy here," I said.

"I think so too," he said. "I've always wanted a place by the sea."

Dad dropped me at home after we'd thoroughly explored the house, then he went off to seal the deal with Dan. Mum was in the living room tidying up when I got in, so I went through to talk to her.

"Okay, Mum, you have three choices," I said. "Lesbian, nun, or Mr. Riley the newsagent."

Mum laughed. "And they're my choices for what?"

"The rest of your life. I think you should get out and start dating."

"Dating!"

"Yes. You're too young to be single."

Mum scratched her head. "Mr. *Riley*? But he's ancient."

"I know. I was only joking about him and being a nun or lesbian. Although I wouldn't object, if that's really the way you want to go. Marie Ferguson in Year Eleven at school, her mum ran off with one of the dinner ladies, so it does happen. . . ."

Mum looked at me in amazement. "Er, hold on.

Rewind a moment. One minute it's out with the photo albums and get back with your father and now it's get out there and start dating. What's happened?"

"I had a talk with Dad. He . . . well . . . I understand a bit better now and I want to say that I'm sorry. I've been an absolute pig and selfish and only thinking of myself and been blaming you and it wasn't your fault that your and dad's feelings changed. And I know you must have been upset because it's not easy breaking up. So, I'm sorry. And I want you to know that I want you to be happy and that I won't be horrible anymore—at least not if I can help it."

Mum laughed, but her eyes were full of tears. She held out her arms to me and I went to her for a hug. "Me too. I know I've been . . . strained lately. But . . . well, we'll get through this. All of us."

"I know," I said. "Because we're all grown-ups."

Mum laughed again and squeezed me harder. "As long as we're all talking—that's what counts. We're still a family—you, me, and Dad—even if we do live in different places."

"I know. I know that now."

"Er, Becca . . . thanks for your suggestions about the dating, but I don't want anyone else. I really don't. It's way too early to be thinking about anything like that. And you do know that's not why we split up—to be with other people?"

"I know. Dad explained and I understand. Sort of."

Mum reached out and took my hand. "Good. And I'm glad we're friends again."

I gave her another hug and thought about what Cat had said about only having one mum and how Cat would never have moments like this in her life and my eyes filled with tears.

"Oh God, here we go again," I said as I sniffed back the tears. "More blub time. It's all I seem to be doing today, whether I'm sad or happy, which is weird."

"It is possible to cry from happiness," said Mum. "It's like the ice in you has melted and is coming out your eyes."

And that made me cry even harder. Best get it all out, I thought. It can't be healthy having great, almighty ice cubes in your chest.

Maker Festival

ONE DAY TO GO.

Two days of rock. Twenty bands.

It was going to be a blast.

On the first night, Dad dropped me off at the main tent where we had all arranged to meet. Everyone was there—Nesta, TJ, Izzie, Lucy, Steve, Lal, Lia, Cat, Mac, and Squidge. Squidge had already got our tickets and was waving them at me as I got out of the car. The lineup for the evening was the Redfoot Sisters, the Pukka Princes, Jason and the Butler Boys, and Jess Rider. Some less famous bands had already been on in the afternoon, so by the time we got in, the tent was already jam-packed and the atmosphere was rocking. As we trailed in, I caught Steve looking at me. I smiled back, but he looked away quickly as if I'd caught him out. I was about to say something to him when Lal put his arm around me and steered me away. I couldn't help but think that it was a shame that Steve hadn't been on the beach that day my mates had dared me to kiss the first boy who came along. As well as being cute, he looked interesting and I would have enjoyed the chance to get to know him and find out what was going on behind his cool demeanor.

"Wow," said Cat as we stood on the sidelines and stared at the assortment of people moving to the music. There were aging hippies in flowing robes, dancing barefoot, motorbike boys in leathers and tattoos, one guy on stilts in a clown's outfit, another guy in a Superman costume, teens like us, parents, even old Mr. Riley was there, grooving away in his own bubble.

"If you can't beat them, join them," said Izzie and pulled me on to the dance floor, where not long after we were joined by the others. We were soon lost in the music and danced our socks off as band after band took their place on the stage. Like Lia, Nesta was a brilliant dancer and boys stood open-mouthed, staring in admiration at the two of them. They looked stunning together, Lia with her long, white-blond hair and Nesta with her long, black, silk hair. People also stared at Squidge, but for a different reason—not one to be held back by his injuries, he was also on the dance floor, looking like some strange half human, half insect thing with his plaster cast and crutches. People were giving him a wide berth, not because he was a brilliant dancer, but for fear that they may get hit by a flying crutch. Mac, Lal, and Steve joined in the dancing too and, for once, Lal wasn't all over me. It was as if he'd finally sensed that I'd cooled off and he didn't want to push it with me. I noticed Steve watching me a couple of times, but as soon as our eyes connected, he'd look away really fast. I hope he didn't think I was a bad person because I kept watching him when I was supposed to be with his brother. I couldn't help it—my eyes kept being drawn back to him. It wasn't as if I was going to do anything about it. I wouldn't do anything to hurt Lal's feelings.

At the end of the evening, all the girls came back to my house for a sleepover, and to help me decide what to wear for the number that Izzie and I were going to do the next night. I wanted to look my best, as we'd be performing in front of so many people—fellow musicians as well as the public. Since the night of Lia's sleepover when we'd agreed to do a song, Izzie and I had spent every hour we could rehearsing. Every single day, singing at my house, in cars, on buses, on the beach—everywhere we could as we didn't have much time left before the big day. We tried all sorts of songs—the ones that I had been practicing and some of Izzie's. Her lyrics were awesome. She'd written songs about every- thing—about hating her mum, loving her mum, food, kisses, friendship, boys, a brilliant rap about school, sad songs, funny songs, happy songs. After we'd sung a selection to our mates and family, everyone, including Lia's dad, said that we sounded best when we sang one of Izzie's, with her playing the guitar. The song was called "Cosmic Kisses," and our voices harmonized really well on it. The whole experience was so different from when I'd sung in the *Pop Princess* competition, where it was all about competing with other contestants. With Izzie, and Mr. Axford on hand to advise, I felt like a proper singer. A professional. And it was way more enjoyable, like we were doing it for us, not for a panel of judges.

Izzie really understood about the need to rehearse and I taught her all the vocal exercises that the competition coaches had taught me. In turn, she told me about how she wrote her songs. She asked to see mine, but I didn't want to put her through the embarrassment of having to fake it like Cat, Mac, Lia, and Squidge all tried to do. Reading her stuff had only confirmed what I already knew— that I was no songwriter. Izzie was though. It seemed to come so naturally to her. I decided I wouldn't bother writing songs anymore. Cat and the gang would be well relieved and, to tell the truth, I felt relieved too. Deep down I knew my songs were bad. I could still sing, though. Nothing would ever put me off that.

I was just going through my wardrobe with the girls when there was a noise at my window.

"What was that?" asked Lucy, who was busy laying out various combinations of tops, dresses, and jeans on my bed.

"Who, more like," I said. "Sounded like someone threw a stone against the glass."

I went to the window and peeped out from behind the curtain. Lal Lovering was standing in the garden below.

Nesta peeked over my shoulder, then darted back out of sight. "Sshhh. Don't let him know that we're here," she whispered.

I pulled back the curtain a little way, then opened the window. Behind me, the girls gathered in a line by the wall to listen.

"Becca . . ." called Lal in a loud whisper.

"You can't come in," I whispered back. "It's past eleven. I'll get into trouble."

"I don't want to come in."

"Oh. What do you want, then?"

Lal shifted about uncomfortably. "Where's your mum? I don't want her to hear."

"She won't. She's in the front room with the telly on. You don't have to whisper, but she wouldn't like it if I let you in."

Lal shifted about again. "Okay. I'm just going to say it, right? Look, I'm not stupid. I've been round the block a few times and, although I don't understand girls, I do know a bit about them."

"And?" Behind me, the girls were doing their best to be quiet, but I could see that Lucy's shoulders had started to shake and she was in danger of bursting out laughing.

"I can tell you've cooled off me. Yeah, I know that you're having a hard time at the moment, but I think it's more than that and . . . well . . . if you want me to hang out with you, then I will. I'm not someone to abandon a mate in time of trouble but . . . well, it is my holiday and . . ."

"I know and that's why I'm not going to dump you or anything."

"But that's just it. No need to be noble on my account, believe me."

"So what, then? Why are you here?"

Lal slumped over so that his arms hung in front of him and he swung them in a cross-cross motion a couple of times.

I laughed. "You're here to do monkey impersonations?"

"Oh God," whispered Lucy. "He's doing that

arm-swinging thing, isn't he? He always does that when he's nervous." I turned to look at her and she swung her arms in front of her in exactly the way Lal was doing it outside. I nodded and then turned back to the window. Lal had stopped the swinging.

"Shazza," he said.

"Shazza?"

Lal nodded. "I think it may be . . . love. I bumped into her in the village a couple of days ago and at the bus stop today, and . . . well to be honest"—he started with the swinging arms again—"there's some serious chemistry happening and I've only got a few days of my hols left and I can sense that you've lost interest. . . . I can tell when a girl's into me and when she's not, and Shazza is and you aren't. So, is it okay if I hang out with her for the rest of the holiday?"

I turned to look at the girls. Lia and Cat were nodding like maniacs and giving me the thumbs-up.

"I think they'll make a really good couple," whispered Cat. "Perfect."

I leaned out of the window. "Sure. Course. Go for it. And we'll be mates, yeah?"

Lal grinned widely. "Yeah. Definitely. Cool."

At that point, Lucy pulled back the curtain. "And what do you think that you're doing prowling around in a girl's garden in the pitch dark?" she demanded in a school-matronly voice.

TJ appeared beside her. "Yes, you're a very, *very* naughty boy!"

Nesta appeared and leaned out of the window next to me. "And you're going to have to be punished!"

Lal groaned and sank to his knees. "Oh nooooo. Don't tell me. Izzie's up there too, isn't she? I'd forgotten you guys were having a sleepover."

Lia swished back the other curtain and all the girls appeared with cheeky grins and waved at him.

"Noooo*oooo*." He thumped his forehead, then threw his arms up in the air in despair. "No. No. No. Nooooo. For God's sake! You lot. You're like a nightmare that follows me everywhere!"

We all started laughing and luckily so did he.

Nesta leaned further out of the window and I had to hang on to her so that she didn't fall out. "Go now, sweet Romeo," she said. "Go and find thy true love. Go to thy Shazza with words of poetry and . . ."

Lal got up and made a rude gesture at her with

his hands. "Oh get lost, Nesta Williams," he said, then he turned and slouched into the shadows and out of the garden.

"So, Becca," said Cat as soon as I'd closed the window. "Are you going to pursue Steve now? I saw you eyeing him up all night."

"Oh yeah?" said Lucy. "What's all this?"

"Becca fancies your other brother now," said Cat.

"Oh, tell everyone my secrets, why don't you?" I said as I clamped my hand over her mouth and pushed her down on to the bed. "You must be silenced."

"So, do you?" asked TJ.

I let Cat up and turned to face the rest of the girls. "Yeah but . . . no. Okay, a bit. But he's Lal's brother. And yours, Lucy. I wouldn't do it to Lal. Even though we finished and everything, I wouldn't want to hurt him."

"Oh, he won't mind," said Lucy. "I've known him longer than you have, don't forget. As long as he's got someone. He's all for trying out as many people as possible before he settles down—his words, not mine. I wouldn't worry at all. Really. He and one of his mates used to have a competition back in London where they had a chart on the back of Lal's bedroom door and if either of them pulled, they got a gold star. So don't feel bad, Becca. I've no doubt that Lal liked you, but I wouldn't be surprised if you end up as a gold star on his door as well. Lal likes to try his luck and fancies himself as a bit of a player. Steve, on the other hand, is totally different. I think you should go for it with him. He treats girls like the intelligent individuals they are, not contenders for the gold-star chart. I think you and he would really get on."

I shook my head. "No, I don't think so," I said. "It's too soon. And anyway, I don't think he even likes me. Every time I catch his eye, he looks away. It's weird—like with some boys, you get an idea of how they see you. With Steve, I have no idea how he sees me at all."

"He does like you," said TJ. "I saw him watching you dance this evening. He definitely likes you."

"Get him to take a photo of you and then you'll find out if he likes you or not," said Lucy. "He's into portrait photography and often you can tell what he thinks of his subject by how he captures them."

"Yeah. He doesn't show his feelings the way Lal does," said Izzie. "The two of them are like chalk and cheese. Lal is an open book. What you see is what you get. No hidden depths. You always know exactly where you are with him. Steve is much harder to read."

"But worth the effort, if you're willing to make it," said TJ. "He and I had a thing for a while before I met Luke and I can honestly say that he is a really great guy."

"So, what happened?" I asked.

Izzie, Nesta, and Lucy chorused, "Luuuuuuke."

"She found her soul mate," said Izzie.

"Hey, if you fall in love with Steve and marry him, then we'd be sisters as well as mates," said Lucy.

I laughed. "Hey, give me a break. We've hardly even spoken to each other yet."

"And we could all be bridesmaids," said Nesta as Izzie and TJ lined up next to her.

"And us too," said Lia and Cat, who lined up with them.

Izzie started singing, *"Here comes the bride, here comes the briiiide . . ."*

Nesta put her hands together as if she was carrying an imaginary bouquet and the others quickly caught on and copied her and started walking toward me. They looked totally mad.

"Ohmigod, scary!" I said, laughing. "The attack of the zombie bridesmaids."

That was a cue for them to roll their eyes back and pull their best horror faces while Nesta let out a low groan. "Wuhoooooooo. They were dead. But they were deadly. *Killer Bridesmaids.* Coming to a wedding near you soooooooon."

"Not listening, not listening," I said as I plugged my ears with my fingers. "Now I'll never be able to talk to Steve without picturing you lot in front of me being stupid."

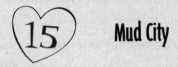

Mud City

"OH NOOOOOOOOOOO . . ." groaned Lia as she pulled back the curtain the next morning.

I didn't have to get out of bed to see why she had groaned. Although it was nine o'clock, the sky was black and I could hear the sound of rain lashing against the window.

"Poo buckets," said Cat. "So much for our sunny summer festival."

A knock at the door announced Mum carrying mugs of tea on a tray. She came in and set the tray down on the cabinet next to the bed. "The forecast isn't too good for later either," she said. "I don't think it's going to clear."

Izzie, Nesta, TJ, and Lucy, who had been sleeping in the spare room next door appeared and soon we were all squashed into my bed with our feet under the duvet, Cat, Lia, and I sitting at the top and the others at the bottom.

"A bit of rain won't put us off," said Izzie as she sipped her tea. "We're British!"

"And bonkers!" added Lucy just as there was a flash of lightning outside, followed soon after by a low boom of thunder.

"But will anyone actually turn up in this?" asked Nesta.

"Of course," said Cat. "Most people have a two-day ticket and we'll be in the tent. It will be fine. All we need is a pair of wellies."

"Hhmm . . . very sexy. Not," said Nesta.

"Depends how you wear them," said Lucy.

"I was thinking of on my head," said Nesta.

"I don't know why you're even worried," said TJ. "You'd look sexy in a bin bag."

"I was hoping to wear my strappy sandals," said Nesta.

"Me too," I said. "But I don't think they'd be right in this rain."

"Oh, for heaven's sake," said Cat. "You're acting like a right bunch of wet drip—er, okay, wrong analogy. Precious princesses. Get a grip. A bit of rain?

We can still dress up. We get a lift up there in our wellies and rain gear, get into the tent, then it's off with the anoraks to reveal the goddesses we are underneath."

Nesta nodded. "Geek to goddess in one change. Cool."

After breakfast, all the girls except Izzie disappeared to get ready and Izzie and I spent a few hours running through our song. Izzie had brought her gear with her last night, so she could get changed with me and we could go up together.

At the allotted time, we donned our singing outfits. We had decided to keep it really simple and went with similar outfits—jeans, little camisole tops with lace edging, leather belts slung low over our hips, and cowboy boots. Her outfit was all black; mine white. We had to borrow some things from the other girls to make it work. The jeans were our own, but Cat lent Izzie a black top, TJ lent me a white one, Nesta lent Izzie a fab black leather belt with a silver buckle, and Lia lent me a white one with diamante studs. I had my white cowboy boots from Prague and Izzie had cowboy boots that she'd bought on the King's Road in London.

When we'd finished dressing and faffing about with hairdryers and makeup, we stood side by side in front of the long mirror in the hall downstairs.

"You look *faaaan*tastic," said Dad, who had arrived earlier to be our chauffeur.

Mum came out to join him. She nodded. "Beautiful. Let me a take a picture."

It was good to see Mum and Dad together. Both of them seemed relaxed and at ease with each other and, even though a part of me would have preferred it if we were living together still, another part was beginning to accept that this was how it was going to be from now on. I understood that we *were* still a family. Nothing could ever change that. And some days, like today, we'd do stuff together like we used to. We just didn't live under the same roof anymore. And I couldn't deny that both of them seemed happier, like some of the strain from the last few months had lifted. Mum was in jeans for a change and she looked pretty with her hair loose on her shoulders.

When Dad went out to bring the car round, I looked out at the unrelenting rain, then down at my outfit. "Maybe we should both have gone for black," I said to Izzie. "You'll be okay if you get covered in mud. White wasn't such a great idea."

Mum handed me my wellies and raincoat. "Just get these on until you're inside the tent and you'll be fine."

I put on the coat, wellies and my baseball cap, found my umbrella, and made a dash for the car. Soon the four of us were on our way up to Maker once again.

"We're singing in the rain," Dad sang as the rain continued to come down in buckets.

"Just singing in the rain," Mum joined in with him.

Up at the festival site, the car park was jammed with cars, the drivers trying not to let their tires get stuck in the field that was fast turning to mud. Dad found a spot in the corner on some grass and we scrambled out and sloshed our way across to the main tent. The site was a total washout—a disaster area, with tents blown away and a multitude of wet people slopping about in wet-weather gear. We made our way over to a stall selling tea and bacon sandwiches near the main entrance, where we had arranged to meet the others. They were all huddled under a couple of umbrellas and dressed like Izzie and me in raincoats and assorted caps and hats to keep off the rain.

"Ah, the British summer," TJ said with a laugh as we joined them.

"Poor campers," said Cat when she saw me looking around at the sea of mud.

"Actually, no one seems that bothered," said TJ as a guy wearing only a T-shirt and boxers slid past on his backside in the mud. He was followed by a bunch of his mates. All of them had mud smeared over their faces. Another guy was entertaining people with juggling. At various spots around the site, people were sitting with drums or guitars, singing and playing under umbrellas or makeshift tents. Some people had given up trying to stay dry and had simply got soaked through—it was wet, but it wasn't cold.

"We got here early and had a look round," said Cat. "People have been having a right laugh."

"I wouldn't want to be camping," said Nesta with a haughty sniff. "Give me a five-star hotel and hot water any day. Camping is so not my style."

"Nor mine," I said. "I'd be with you, Nesta—in big white fluffy towels, all dry and warm."

"Room service," she said, smiling back.

"Minibar," I said. We were so on the same level.

I took a peek inside the main tent as the others finished their bacon sandwiches and saw that TJ had been right. It didn't seem to matter that it was raining outside. Amid the earthy smell of mud and wet bodies and clothes drying off, everyone looked happy enough, and the place was rocking to the sound of Blue Monday up on the stage. I took a leaflet from a guy dressed in a kilt and glanced at the lineup: The Local Heroes, Donkey Boys, Jellied Eels, Pelican Moon, and Manic Zone had been on already. After Blue Monday, it was Club 4, the Lady Rebels, Izzie and me (we were billed simply as Izzie Foster and Becca Howard), Big Minging Momma, and then the grand finale, Sambuca, an eight-piece Latin groove ensemble.

My stomach seemed full of a thousand butterflies as I looked around and thought about the fact that within the next hour, I had to get up on stage and sing.

Suddenly I felt someone nudge me in the ribs.

"Eyes left," said Lucy, appearing at my side. "Your poor, sad, ex-boyfriend. He looks soooo upset, like he's missing you soooooo much."

A stab of guilt hit me as I glanced over to where Lucy was looking, then I burst out laughing. In the middle of the dance floor were Lal and Shazza. They had their arms wrapped round each other, eyes closed and totally oblivious to the rest of the world as they snogged away.

"You rotten thing," I said as I play-strangled her. "You had me going for a minute there."

Lucy laughed. "Sorry," she said. "Listen. I've been told to ask you to go back to the main entrance. There are some photographers there from the local paper who want to take some pics of you and Izzie."

"Oh, right," I said and turned to go.

"Better take off your rain gear," said Lucy. "They won't want to snap you in that."

I took off my mac and cap, gave them to Lucy, and dashed back to the main entrance. Izzie looked relieved to see me and grabbed my hand.

"I was wondering where you'd got to. They want

some pics of us outside in the rain with the hills and clouds in the distance. We should be okay if you tread carefully and we keep our umbrellas up."

"Should I change into my white boots?" I asked.

Izzie shook her head. "No. Keep your wellies on. They'll probably only do a head-and-shoulders shot."

The photographer was beckoning to us, so we went out to meet him and he positioned us by a fence to the left of the main tent. As he snapped away, I noticed that Steve Lovering was busy taking photos of his own. To our right, the bunch of lads that we'd seen earlier with mud-smeared faces had now stripped off down to their underwear and were totally caked with mud from head to toe as they rolled and slid about in the puddles.

By this time, I had goose pimples all over, the rain was still lashing down and, even though we had the umbrella up, the rain was coming down at an angle and my jeans and top were getting wetter by the minute. I was glad I hadn't worn my white boots, as they would have been totally ruined.

When the photographer had finished, he thanked

us then turned to go and join Steve, who was taking shots of the boys larking about in the mud.

"Let's get back inside," urged Izzie.

I turned to follow her, but as I did, one of the mud boys slid down the hill and straight into the back of my knees. I buckled immediately on the impact, lost my grip on the umbrella, and went flying. The umbrella flew off in a sudden gust of wind and I hit the ground, the boy landing on top of me a split second later.

"Ohmigod!" cried Izzie as she tried to push him off and help me up.

Another strong gust of wind blew her umbrella inside out and the boy she was trying to move aside slipped onto his back and his feet hit her on the side of the legs. Then she lost her balance and toppled on top of me.

"Sorry, sorry," the boy blustered as I tried to get onto my knees. Izzie reached out to me and the boy tried to scramble away up the slope, but he slid back into us and knocked us both over again so that we were all lying on top of each other in a heap of wet bodies.

By this time, the rain had plastered my hair to my face and I could feel the sting of my mascara as it began to run down my cheeks. Izzie tried to get up again, but slipped further down the grassy hill and straight into a huge puddle of mud. Her mascara was also running and her hair stuck to her face, and there was mud smeared on her bare arms.

Izzie sat up, groaned, and looked at her watch. "Oh, Christ," she said. "We're on in ten minutes. . . ."

I looked up at the sky, then around at the faces staring down at us with dismay. I glanced down at my clothes. My gorgeous white outfit was now dark brown.

"I told you I should have worn black," I said as all my dreams of looking my glamorous best on stage drained away. I glanced over at Izzie, my sodden fellow rock chick, and burst out laughing.

Izzie burst out laughing too. As the rain continued to pelt down, we both turned our faces up to the sky, rose to our knees, opened our arms to the skies and let the rain wash over us.

"If you can't beat them, join them," said Izzie.

I suddenly became aware of Steve Lovering snapping away. So now I know how he sees me—a mud-colored fool. . . . Talk about humiliation, I thought, as he zoomed his camera in on me. How could I have ever imagined that he might fancy me? Well, I hoped he was having a good laugh as I tried to get up, slipped again and mud oozed through my fingers.

A few moments later, Izzie dragged me to my feet and, looking like two pathetic wet drips, we trooped back into the main tent.

Mac came running toward us. He looked horrified at our appearance. "Ohmigod. What happened? Zac's looking for you. You're on next. You can't go on like that. . . . You're covered in mud."

"Oh really," I said. "I hadn't noticed!"

"It's the new look," said Izzie. "And we haven't got time to change."

"What are you going to do?" asked Mac.

"The show must go on," I said.

Izzie nodded. "Lead the way," she said and together we dripped our way up to the front.

Zac took one look at us and burst out laughing.

"Don't ask," I said.

"Yeah, mud is the new black," said Izzie. "It's the Queen Boudicca warrior look."

"Very fetching and most authentic," said Zac. "Up you go, then. . . ."

We made our way up onto the stage and stood at the microphones. A stunned silence fell in the tent.

"Er . . . a funny thing happened on the way here," Izzie started.

"And nobody can say that we don't muck in," I said.

"People have been asking what our stage name is," said Izzie. "We didn't know until just now but we've decided to call ourselves the Sludge Buckets."

Stage right, Zac clapped, then called out, "Let's hear it for the Sludge Buckets!"

At the back, I could see Mac, Squidge, and the others laughing and then they began to cheer. Soon the whole tent was cheering us. I turned to look at Izzie. She looked a total mess. Water was still dripping down her face in tiny rivulets. She looked over at me and burst out laughing. It felt exhilarating to be up there in front of so many people, not caring a blot about what I looked like. I was covered in mud, my makeup had run, and somewhere along the way, I suddenly realized, I had managed to lose one of my wellies.

Izzie reached behind to the back of the stage where Zac had left her guitar ready for her. She slung it over her shoulder and began to play the opening chords to "Cosmic Kisses." I took a deep breath, waited for my cue, and then we both began to sing.

> *"I'm sending you cosmic kisses straight from*
> *my heart;*
> *A planet collision won't tear us apart.*
> *The distance between us is never too far;*
> *I'll hitch a ride on a comet to get where*
> *you are."*

The following morning, I got a call from Izzie.

"Have you seen the paper?" she asked.

"No. Why?"

"There's a photo of you on the front."

"Me? But the guy took photos of both of us. . . ."

"Yeah. There are some more inside—loads from the festival, but the one on the front is of you on your own and it was taken when we were swimming in the mud."

Oh God, I thought as I raced downstairs to find the paper. It's going to be so humiliating. I'll be the laughing stock of my year when I go back to school in September. I can just hear their comments: Failed in *Pop Princess* and now look at her . . . Oh God.

The paper was lying on the mat in the hall and I picked it up, took a deep breath, and prepared myself for looking a fool. The shot of me took up a quarter of the page. But it wasn't awful.

It was fabulous!

I looked like I was having the time of my life. My head was thrown back, my face turned up to the sky. The caption underneath read *Mud Princess*.

Mum came down the stairs in her dressing gown and looked over my shoulders, then blinked. "Wow," she said. "That's you. . . . You look beautiful, Bec—really beautiful. Free and wild. That's possibly the best picture I've ever seen of you. You *have* to get me a copy of the photograph." She screwed up her eyes to read the name of the photographer.

"Steve someone," she said as she strained to read the small print.

I took the paper back from her and read the name. *Steve Lovering*, it said. Steve Lovering?

For a moment I didn't know what to think. I went into the kitchen and put on the kettle to make Mum and myself a cup of tea and looked at the other photos from the festival. There was a whole selection, some by Steve, some by the man who had photographed Izzie and me before we fell over.

As the kettle was boiling, I heard the sound of the doorbell and Mum opening the door. A moment later, she appeared in the kitchen.

"There's a boy at the front door who says he's got your welly. He says you lost it last night," she added, then started laughing. "It's not exactly a glass slipper and he's not exactly dressed as a prince, but he does look charming."

I went out into the hall.

It was Steve.

Look for the last

truth or dare?

featuring the Mates, Dates characters!

All Mates Together

"HEY CAT, HE'S a cutie," said Nesta as she got up and pulled me with her.

It was so weird. I'd been looking forward to seeing Jamie again for ages. Imagining how it would be. Where it would be. But now that it was actually happening, I wanted the ground to open up and swallow me. It was all a big mistake. I looked like a total prat. Why on earth had I let the girls talk me into this, never mind wearing this mad wig? There was no guarantee at all that Jamie would find it a laugh—in fact, he might not even be pleased to see me. As I watched him approach us, I realized that I actually didn't know him that well at all. We had only spent a couple of hours together on the trip to Morocco and, although he had seemed like a nice guy and was keen on me there, he looked much more sophisticated than I remembered. I knew he went to private school, but now that I'd glimpsed where he lived, as well, I could see that we were from very different worlds. He was going to think this whole idea was so childish. Oh God, oh God, never again, I thought as we began to walk toward him. Already he was staring—and who could blame him? I thought as I began to blush as pink as TJ's wig.

"Actually, I don't want him to see me like this," I whispered, and tried to steer the girls off in another direction while at the same time hiding my face so that he wouldn't see me. Hopefully with the sunglasses and the wig, he wouldn't recognize me at all and we could get back to TJ's and forget the whole thing.

Too late. He was making a beeline for us.

"Hey, girls," he said as he got closer. "It's a bit early for the Notting Hill carnival."

"Vot carnival do you speak of, Eengleesh boy?" drawled Nesta in a heavy Russian-ish accent.

"I thought we were being Scottish," said TJ in a perfect Irish accent.

Jamie looked like he was going to burst out laughing—and then he saw me and squinted his eyes as if to focus more. As expected, he did a double take. Then he came closer. "You look like someone I . . . hey . . . Cat, is that you under there?"

"Cat? Me? No. Probably someone who looks like me. . . . I mean, her. . . ." I blustered.

"Surprise," chorused TJ and Nesta.

"Yeah—surprise," I said. "I . . . we . . . that is . . ."

I couldn't deny the fact that Jamie looked delighted and immediately wrapped me in a big bear hug. "Cat Kennedy! This is fantastic. Wow . . . but you look . . . strange."

I was lost for words, caught between being happy to see him and wondering if I ought to explain.

Luckily Nesta took over. "We've heard a lot about you," she said. "I'm Nesta, and this is my mate, TJ. And, er . . . I couldn't possibly use your loo, could I? I'm dying to go."

Jamie looked totally bemused. "Loo? What? Er . . . oh . . ." he stuttered as he glanced nervously back at the house. "Er . . ."

Nesta crossed her knees and clasped her hands in the praying position. "Pleeeeease . . ."

Jamie's expression changed from looking delighted to being anxious. He looked studiously at our wigs and then finally nodded. "Come on then, but . . . listen . . . er . . . yeah, great look and all that—but would you mind taking your wigs off before we go in?"

Nesta, TJ, and I exchanged glances as if to say, What's the problem? but we whipped the wigs off all the same and stashed them in TJ's rucksack. As Jamie ushered us back to the house he glanced at me, but his expression was now impenetrable and I began to wish that I'd never come.

By the bestselling author of the Mates, Dates series,

Cathy Hopkins

Meet Cat, Becca, Squidge, Mac, and Lia. These girls and guys are totally tight—and totally obsessed with the game of truth or dare . . . even when it reveals too much!

Every book is a different dare . . . and a fun new adventure.

Read them all:

White Lies and Barefaced Truths

The Princess of Pop

Teen Queens and Has-Beens

Starstruck

Double Dare

Midsummer Meltdown

Love Lottery

All Mates Together
(featuring all the Mates, Dates girls)

From Simon Pulse
Published by Simon & Schuster

WANTED

Single Teen Reader in search of a FUN romantic comedy read!

How NOT to Spend Your Senior Year
CAMERON DOKEY

Royally Jacked
NIKI BURNHAM

Ripped at the Seams
NANCY KRULIK

Cupidity
CAROLINE GOODE

Spin Control
NIKI BURNHAM

South Beach Sizzle
SUZANNE WEYN &
DIANA GONZALEZ

She's Got the Beat
NANCY KRULIK

30 Guys in 30 Days
MICOL OSTOW

Animal Attraction
JAMIE PONTI

A Novel Idea
AIMEE FRIEDMAN

Scary Beautiful
NIKI BURNHAM

Getting to Third Date
KELLY McCLYMER

Dancing Queen
ERIN DOWNING

Major Crush
JENNIFER ECHOLS

Do-Over
NIKI BURNHAM

Love Undercover
JO EDWARDS

Prom Crashers
ERIN DOWNING

Gettin' Lucky
MICOL OSTOW

Available from Simon Pulse **Published by Simon & Schuster**